UNSAID GOODBYE TO MY UNFORGETTABLE FATHER

A HEARTFELT STORY ABOUT MY INCREDIBLE FATHER AND CIRCUMSTANCES THAT PREVENTED ME FROM SAYING A PROPER GOODBYE TO HIM.

RENE SAMUEL

Made with ♥ on the Notion Press Platform
www.notionpress.com

This heartfelt dedication is in honour of my beloved late father, Samuel Prabakar. He was more than just a parent to me; he was my mentor and guiding light. Like a compass, he navigated me through the twists and turns of life, illuminating the path ahead. His teachings went beyond the confines of a classroom; they were practical life lessons that equipped me with the skills to face the world head-on. I vividly recall the day he taught me how to change a flat tire. With hands weathered by years of hard work, he gently guided mine, imparting not only car repair knowledge but also self-reliance. His lessons in the kitchen transcended mere cooking; they were about creating an atmosphere of warmth and love, nurturing and caring for those around us. But beyond these tangible skills, my father instilled in me values that have become the very foundations of my character. Honesty was non-negotiable, as he would often emphasize. He ingrained in me the significance of being truthful not only to others but also to myself. Respect was another virtue close to his heart - "Treat others as you wish to be treated," he would repeatedly remind me. And then there was his unwavering belief in hard work. He exemplified that nothing worth having comes without effort. Through his dedication, persistence, and never-give-up attitude, he showed me that dreams can be achieved with perseverance alone. Every conversation with him felt like a valuable lesson; every interaction became an opportunity for personal growth. He taught me the art of attentive listening, the power of empathy, and the virtue of patience. I learned from him that kindness is not a weakness but rather a strength to be cherished above all else - love being its most powerful manifestation. In essence, my father was not only my greatest teacher but also my guide on how to live life well. His invaluable lessons have shaped and moulded me into the person I am today. This dedication is a tribute to you, Dad.

Contents

Author's Biography *vii*

Foreword *xi*

Preface *xiii*

Acknowledgements *xv*

Prologue *xvii*

1. Every Journey In Life Starts With A Melody 1
2. Flashback 7
3. When Mom Met Dad 11
4. Questioning Dad's Self Destruction Habits 17
5. Making A Deal With Dad 25
6. A Night Of Horror 30
7. Mom Returns 37
8. Mom Discovers A Second Chance At Love 41
9. Worst Day Of My Life 51
10. Rest In Peace Dad 57
11. After Dad 64
12. Dazzling Diamond Ring. Mr Right 77
13. Throwback To 6th Grade 86
14. Mathematics - The Ultimate Nemesis. 100
15. Love Assignment 108
16. Confession 112
17. Sundays 115
18. My True Feelings 124

Thank you, my reader. 135

AUTHOR'S BIOGRAPHY

Rene Samuel - 10/05/1996

In a world where boundaries often confine us, there are individuals who refuse to be limited by the constraints of a singular path. One such individual is Rene Samuel, whose journey is an inspiring tale of pursuing multiple dreams simultaneously and proving that it's never too late to make aspirations a reality.

Rene's journey begins with an exceptional academic achievement - a Triple Major Bachelor of Arts Degree in

Psychology, Physical Education, and Travel and Tourism from Mount Carmel College in Bangalore, India. This diverse educational background laid the foundation for her multifaceted approach to life.

From a young age, Rene had an unwavering passion for writing and storytelling. She understood the magic of words in transforming and inspiring individuals. This passion led her to embark on a career as a Freelance Writer and Audio Content Curator after college. She created engaging blogs and captivating illustrations for various platforms, showcasing her expertise in creative writing and storytelling.

Rene's book titled "Unsaid Goodbye To My Unforgettable Father" is a deeply personal and heart-wrenching journey. It explores the painful reality of losing her father to suicide while also shining a glimmer of hope as her mother discovers a second chance at love. This book serves as a poignant reminder that even in life's darkest moments, there is potential for healing and rediscovery.

Becoming a published author was not without its challenges for Rene. She faced rejections from publishers at a young age but held onto her book draft with hopes of one day realizing her dream. Ten years later, her perseverance pays off as Notion Press accepts her book, proving that dreams can indeed come true with determination and maturity.

Rene's journey extends beyond writing; she also works as an IT technical support professional where she combines both her creative and technical expertise. Her role requires exceptional communication skills and product knowledge to provide top-notch service to clients. This duality allows her to approach scenarios with a unique perspective and problem-solving skills.

But Rene's pursuits don't stop there; she is actively involved in animal welfare activities and even offers pet boarding services. Additionally, she aspires to be a freelance model, adding an exciting dimension to her already dynamic life.

Rene's life philosophy revolves around empowerment. She firmly believes in embracing opportunities and pursuing multiple dreams simultaneously, emphasizing that settling for just one dream limits one's true potential.

The story of Rene Samuel serves as a testament to the importance of resilience, determination, and believing in oneself. It showcases the idea that life is too short to confine oneself to a single dream. Her journey inspires us all to break free from conventional thinking and embrace the countless opportunities that life presents.

Rene Samuel's story is an inspiration for anyone seeking to pursue their dreams and passions in a world brimming with possibilities.

FOREWORD

Life itself resembles a storybook—an ongoing narrative where we are both authors and protagonists—where each day presents new chapters filled with challenges, choices, and journeys yet untaken. Our task is to seize these opportunities, to make each moment meaningful and impactful, and to live life to its fullest potential. By doing so, we transform our existence into a remarkable story, one that fills us with pride and inspires others in turn.

In an increasingly harsh world, be the change you wish to see - become someone's guiding light amidst darkness or illuminate your own life by shifting perspectives and embracing new ideas. Stand strong even if standing alone seems daunting; not every promise of forever brings comfort nor does every failed attempt signify the end. You can always try again.

We believe that everything happens for a reason. It's okay to feel weak, to break down, to have unanswered questions, and to experience moments of depression. These emotions remind us that life is worth living. The world offers a variety of experiences like different cuisines with diverse flavours and tastes. Enjoy each one by savouring every moment and embracing new possibilities. Nothing is impossible unless you attempt. As the famous saying goes, "Nothing is impossible; the word itself says 'I'm possible'." Remember, you are the architect of your destiny.

Preface

The passing of my father had a profound impact on me, which led to a transformation within myself. The overwhelming flood of emotions I experienced found solace in the art of writing. It was through this medium that I yearned to express and share my deep insights with the world. This cathartic process revealed the immense power held within my words and their ability to resonate with others. Writing has granted me the extraordinary capability to shape the world around me. My ultimate goal is to empower young children, encouraging them to become independent creators of their own destinies through the captivating stories I tell.

I must confess that I am not without my imperfections. Along my journey, I have encountered countless flaws and experienced numerous trial-and-error moments. However, these experiences have molded me into the person I am today, and that is something I take great pride in. The moments of regret that I have faced have served as valuable lessons, allowing me to grow and evolve into a more resilient individual. In many ways, I am an extension of my father's legacy, carrying on his vision and striving for what he was unable to achieve. As you immerse yourself in the pages of my book, you will embark on a captivating journey filled with unexpected twists and turns that will keep you at the edge of your seat. From moments of despair to overwhelming joy, this narrative will tug at your heartstrings while simultaneously leaving you uplifted with hope for what lies ahead.

Acknowledgements

I would like to express my deepest gratitude to my mother, Sophia Samuel, for the immense love she has bestowed upon me. This love, which knows no bounds and is filled with unwavering support, goes beyond mere consolation and celebration. It encompasses growth, nurturing, and empowerment. It has given me the resilience to confront the challenges of the world and the bravery to pursue my aspirations. Through her love, she has instilled in me a belief that I am capable of accomplishing anything I set my mind to. I am truly thankful for this profound affection that has remained a constant presence in my life. It has not only shaped and moulded me but also defined who I am today. With this steadfast love as my foundation, I have found the determination to persevere, the audacity to dream, and the unwavering faith to follow my heart's desires. Her love served not only as a safety net but also as a launching pad propelling me towards realizing my dreams.

Prologue

In the depths of solitude and fear,
Is there anyone who listens, can you hear?
In the darkness of night, her tears flow,
Longing for someone to be her hero.

Left to face her shame all alone,
Hidden, her true self remains unknown.
Beneath the scars and tear-stained face,
She wonders if acceptance she'll embrace.

Silent in a corner, lost in deep thought,
Questioning why life feels so fraught.
It wasn't her fault, how she came to be,
Forced upon by someone's cruelty.

Perhaps it was a mistake, every mark he made,
Her plea echoes through the heavens' glade.
"Grant me justice and care," she cries aloud,
Innocence shattered amidst every crowd.

I

Every Journey In Life Starts With A Melody

Every journey in life starts with a melody. You know those scenes in movies where everything seems perfect and there's a beautiful song playing in the background? It's like pure magic, and I absolutely adore it. I sometimes wish I could have those moments where I could just play a song to convey my emotions. It would make certain situations much simpler since music holds a special place in my heart.

Music has a unique ability to connect with our emotions and deeply resonate with us. We become deeply attached to certain songs and their lyrics, finding them more captivating than the melody itself. Music plays an incredibly significant role in our lives, revealing the beauty it holds in unexpected ways. Through music, I have discovered countless new things that I never knew existed before. It seems that music is omnipresent, enhancing even the most mundane experiences. Picture walking into a restaurant where the music sets a romantic and enchanting ambiance, effortlessly aligning every element to create a perfect moment - it's almost as if something divine is at play. Music has the power to complete these moments, making them truly magical. Undoubtedly, music offers an exceptional way to spend our leisure time; for many of us, it serves as a profound source of inspiration, joy, and happiness - a means of living life to its fullest. Moreover, music serves as an invaluable teacher throughout our journey in life; it imparts lessons through every experience we encounter. It occupies a significant space in our lives by providing mental and emotional detoxification - transporting us to a world devoid of worries and pain. In times of trouble or distress, music acts as an escape route that helps us transcend difficult situations and find solace beyond them

Music conveys the lyrics where the words that had never been spoken are heard.

We also have a penchant for humming along and sharing a little jig or two with a familiar tune that we deem our 'favourite' and don't feel embarrassed doing. Some artists are not to everyone's taste, and some artists are just not so taken to. For some people, they just love the lyrical content more than the melody; for other people, they crave the soft melodies and that's comforting to their ears; other people are willing to lean into silence. Silence is fine but is there some soul out there who doesn't love music?! It is as necessary as food, clothes, and a home. Are you required to forgo it then? Music is almost like oxygen to our lungs.

Listening to the music and enjoying it with your eyes closed is a wonderful thing.

Just listening to music is like attending a prayer service that forgives your sins. It's so pure and sometimes works like an angel that cleanses every part of your soul turning you into a divine person.

Music isn't something you just listen to, it's something that you relate to by feeling it. That happiness you feel when you listen to a happy song and get that urge to dance to this beat, and also the sad mood when you feel the emotions in the lyrics and the slow tone of the songs that touch your hearts.

We don't just listen to music out of boredom, not that we have it as entertainment; we listen to music because a singing artist becomes our heart and soul.

We associate something with it so that we find ourselves in a world of our own. Sometimes you just want to listen to a song for its lyrics, other times you get attracted by the melody and that song lifts your mood.
Music holds a significant place in our lives. It is not just an art form, but an integral part of our existence. Imagining a world without music is quite eerie, as it fills our surroundings with its enchanting melodies and rhythms. It serves as the perfect motivation to kickstart our day, especially when accompanied by fast-paced beats that energize us instantly. The power of music extends far beyond mere entertainment. It possesses the ability to transform our lives for the better if we harness its potential effectively. By incorporating music into our daily routines, we can create a more productive and balanced lifestyle,

leading to increased happiness and fulfillment. Embracing music should be akin to embracing life itself. Just as life offers us moments of joy and beauty, so does music. When we allow ourselves to immerse in its harmonies, we unlock a world of wonders that enriches every aspect of our existence. So go ahead and let the melodies guide you towards a more vibrant and fulfilling life. Embrace the magic of music, and witness your life blossom into something even more extraordinary!

Bangalore, a city that attracts different kinds of people from all parts of the world, is one of the liveliest destinations in India. This is a city that is known and loved for its climate. During the summer holidays, foreign tourists enjoy sunbathing and getting a few sun rays. More likely you'll notice them walking alone by the pool in swimsuits during summers. Most of them wouldn't want to use sunscreens as they want to get a tan. They enjoy their beautiful monsoon rains with hot samosas and chats. Yep, so like us!

It's September already and I've got myself already experiencing the beautiful monsoon rain and smelling the wet in the atmosphere. It's thrilling and it feels like heaven on earth. Bangalore's weather is blissful and lovely. The monsoon makes it nearly impossible to even step out of the house. Before you do that, you must think; that because the rains are that bad, it could mean we could be struck by a cyclone as a bad tropical storm. We are all going to die because only God's protection can save us from any attack.

My morning started with the sun rising, and its rays slowly

began to filter into my room to rest on my eyes. I opened my eyes with one of those small smiles that make you feel that you have just made a decision that can lead to some positive changes. Flipping over the covers and stretching my arms, I turned towards my left and looked at the watch; 7: at 00 a.m.

"Hello sun, you are so gentle to wake me up with your glow on me—I will gladly take you over any human that would come to bother me while I am in my deep thoughts. How I must admire you! How I love you. You are so beautiful and when you bring your light into our life, it takes away darkness. Some people may not recognize your value, but you need to know that it's you who brought light, warmth, and happiness to each one of us."

Well, some of us don't wake up on the right side of the bed and I have to say, sorry, I do! Yes, I think so, unless you don't know what that phrase 'waking up on the wrong side of the bed' means, and it usually means 'Wake up with a foul temper?' I tend to wake up on the wrong side of the bed only when a human interrupts my peaceful meditation. I do get Hulk angry and punch and kick that stimulus. Mind me, I love sleeping. And to anyone wanting to stop me from sleeping — you can expect a slap in the face!

I poured myself a cup of coffee and went to the balcony. I breathed deeply and smelled my warm coffee. Perfect! I gazed at the breeze which welcomed the dawn as my arms reached out wide and allowed a small smile to form on my lips. It felt warm and lovely. The breeze was simply exhilarating. The air felt fresh and cool. From every corner, the birds emerged and chirped their happiness to be alive.

I sang as well as I ran barefoot on cool wet grass by my house. We howled and the dogs croaked happily along with us. And even bugs were screeching loudly! They must be singing about how lovely life is! Indeed, it is. All of it from the sunshine to the sunset.

So, I stepped outside and enjoyed the sun with my coffee while watching birds in their nest feeding their young ones. I look at them and then smile. Above, crows circled and hovered, filling the air with their ghostly caws. The trees close by howled as their branches shook with the wind, and just watching the beautiful nature every morning was my favourite way to start my day. It gave me energy and it made me feel good. When I was young, my mother used to tell me that if you begin your morning by seeing the sunrise, "You can bring in the light of joy because the sun came out to start the day." And now I knew with certainty what it meant. Happiness happens when the sun is shining, and the art sings its happiness into existence. These words always hit me so hard.

My family isn't perfect, I don't know if it's even dysfunctional, they drive fast posh cars, wear designer clothes and I don't have an hourglass physique. I live in a big house and even though I may not get a ton of likes online, I have a small circle and that circle makes me feel good about myself that's the way we should all live...because it's a circle that does a few things that count. The best part? Little things are often the best things, as they're usually here to stay. My eyes are shut now soaking in everything the creator created as my memory takes me back to my young years.

II

Flashback

You could say that the world is a stage — every individual that roams about on this earth possesses something significant to convey and impart his/her own little piece of story. There's always one thing everyone goes through in their lifetime. It's not something that you've learned but it's what they have put into you all your life. Whether you want to see it, or if you just want to overlook it and not judge.
When it comes to assessing someone's actions and experiences, it is important to have empathy and understanding. It is impossible to truly understand someone's situation unless you have experienced it yourself. Therefore, passing judgment without having firsthand knowledge is unfair. We should refrain from assuming that we know everything about how others feel based solely on their actions.

They speak as if they know my story when they have no clue of what I've been through. However, I can no longer tell everyone, "You know me by my name, not my story," because when they do judge, they will—and eventually karma works its wonders. Every human being is different. Everyone handles things in their own way. We have our own stories. We live our own lives, on a personal level every day. That's what defines us. If we continue to judge others without knowing enough, we bring ruin to ourselves. We're ruining the world. And we're further damaging them.

Imagine someone harbouring strong negative feelings towards Justin Bieber, even going so far as to use derogatory language. However, they may not be aware of the challenges he faced and how hard he had to work to achieve success. Just like anyone else, Justin Bieber is a human being deserving of respect. Who are we to judge or question someone's sexuality? It's essential for us to reflect on our own insecurities before directing hate towards others. Often, when we hate someone, it stems from a place of jealousy - a desire for them to be in our shoes instead. Hate can be seen as jealousy turned inside out.

So what message do you want to convey? Before passing judgment on others like Justin Bieber, remember that you haven't experienced life through their lens. We're all human beings in need of support at times; it takes someone stepping up to lend a hand. Instead of harbouring hatred towards them simply because they haven't wronged us personally, let's focus on spreading positivity.

Let's stop tarnishing individuals like Justin Bieber or anyone else because we don't realize the extent of harm we might cause them. Each person possesses their own unique beauty as creations of God – inherently beautiful in their own right. Everyone has talents and values bestowed upon them; it is our responsibility to discover and express these qualities in the most exquisite manner possible for the world to appreciate.

Certainly, like myself, you must have heard numerous love stories that begin with phrases like "Yeah we met here and there and then we dated for a while and got along so well that we ended up getting married." However, not many individuals marry out of genuine love; rather, they marry out of fear of spending their lives alone. People are infatuated with the concept of marital bliss rather than with the person they are entering into matrimony with. Marriage is a sacred union that binds two individuals together, vowing to stand by each other indefinitely regardless of circumstances. Unfortunately, despite these solemn vows exchanged during marriage ceremonies, unions often crumble under various pressures. I find myself in agreement with Herbert Spencer's sentiments when he wrote: "The present relationship existing between husband and wife, where one claims a command over the actions of the other, is nothing more than a remnant of the old leaven of slavery. It is necessarily destructive of refined love; for how can a man continue to regard as his type of the ideal a being whom he has degraded to something below himself by denying the equality of privilege?"

This prevailing power dynamic within marriages often serves as one common reason behind their dissolution today: when one partner assumes authority over the other. However, I cannot claim this to be the sole reason since every individual is unique and possesses their own set of expectations from marriage—some of which may not align and may contribute to its demise.

Growing up amidst a spectrum ranging from blissful marriages to shattered ones and from healthy relationships to abusive ones has always left me disheartened whenever the subject of romantic involvement arises. I have consistently reassured myself that I will never fall victim to this institution. Identifying as an introverted asexual, I have never engaged in romantic relationships with either gender simply because I have not experienced attraction towards them. The concept of romance does not resonate with me personally. My happiness does not hinge on another person; I am perfectly capable of finding joy within myself.

Certainly, while indulging in a heartfelt love story, I can't help but feel a surge of emotions. After all, emotions are an intrinsic part of the human experience. It's only natural for me to be deeply moved. However, the concept of being in love or having a romantic partner doesn't carry much weight in my personal journey. It simply doesn't align with how I perceive myself and my aspirations.

Making a decision that will have long-lasting consequences and take on more responsibility is no easy task. I've always been taught that it's important to give ourselves enough time to truly understand each other's qualities and build a genuine friendship before diving into a relationship. However, not all relationships work out that way, and sometimes all the effort we put in can go to waste. It's something we have to learn to accept.

Despite the challenges that come with relationships, I consider myself fortunate to have everything I need and desire. In addition to having an abundance of new books waiting to be read, I also find ways to fill the pages of my own life with exciting experiences and adventures. Interestingly enough, even ancient texts like the Bible recount instances of extreme poverty where people were driven to unimaginable measures such as mothers resorting to consuming their own children... It's truly a horrifying reality!

III

When Mom Met Dad

My mom was introduced to my dad through a mutual friend after they both went on a college trip. She soon discovered that my dad was in the garment business and began visiting him frequently with piles of clothes. Dad, being the wonderful gentleman he is, made her feel comfortable in his presence. As time went on, they started opening up about their secrets, deepest desires, goals, and achievements - growing closer with each passing day and building an entirely new connection.

My mom was deeply affected when she learned about my dad's past struggles. She could empathize with the pain and suffering he had endured. It's easy for us to show compassion or pity towards others who have lost parents or experienced abuse during their childhoods - but trying to put ourselves in their shoes gives us a whole new perspective on what they've gone through. It's truly indescribable.

On May 16th, 1990, my parents walked down the aisle together. My mother was only 19 years old at the time while my father was 25. Growing up in India - a traditional country - I initially assumed that my parents had an arranged marriage due to my mother's young age. But I was mistaken; it was a love marriage. The early days of their married life were blissful. However, little did my mother know that my father had a raging alcohol addiction and an unbearable temper.

She decided to marry at a young age to escape a life of poverty and create the luxurious life she had always dreamed of. She believed that with the man she loved by her side, she could provide him with support and encouragement, ultimately bringing about positive change in their lives.

But as fate would have it, there was a twist in their story.

After living together, my mother began experiencing my father's obsession with alcoholism daily - an ongoing torment that she endured. Time flew by without warning, as days turned into months in the blink of an eye. And as time went on, fear and agony became my mother's constant companions. She always held onto hope that my father would change someday, giving him chance after chance - but that change never came. Instead, he continued to sow seeds of pain and destruction.

All I remember is when I found out about my father's alcoholism and uncontrollable temper, I became emotionally numb and distant. He always had a bottle of beer or brandy or vodka in his hand, and there was nothing I could do about it. Looking back now, I often wish I had done something to intervene.

When my brother was born, it brought immense joy not only to my mother but also to our entire family. In Indian culture, having a baby boy is considered a blessing for the household. My brother shared many physical similarities with our father - from his looks to his voice and even his athletic build. He became the second man in our family and was given a first, middle and last name: Reynold Eric Samuel.

My brother plays an incredibly important role in my life - he is my greatest inspiration and a source of strength. I aspire to be like him one day. While there was once a lot of sibling rivalry between us, that eventually reached its peak and subsided.

It was five years after my brother's birth that I entered this family. My mother cherished me as her pride and joy, hoping that I would achieve everything she couldn't. When she looked into my eyes, she saw a reflection of herself and the potential within me. Having parents who love us unconditionally is truly a blessing.

While my brother took after our father in appearance, I inherited my mother's features. From her captivating smile to her defined cheekbones and full lips, I resembled her greatly. Even our slender fingers matched. It's fascinating how two individuals can bear such striking resemblance on the surface yet be so different on the inside, like apples and oranges. Our character traits displayed an opposite pattern: I inherited introversion from my father, while my brother embodied his mother's extroverted nature. The one thing I'm grateful to have inherited from my dad is his eyes, which have been complimented as beautiful countless times, though I've never fully believed it.

Around the time of my 12th birthday, things started to change in our household. My parents began behaving strangely and arguing more frequently than usual. Growing up, I often perceived my dad as an alcoholic most of the time, but when he was sober, he transformed into a loving and caring father without equal. His habits seemed unchangeable; however, out of respect or perhaps fear of uncovering painful truths about his past experiences—I never mustered the courage to ask him why.

🙞

One summer morning during break time, as I sat on the swing on our balcony observing him lean against a wall while smoking and gazing out of the window intently—I finally decided to pose a question that had been lingering within me for an eternity; surprisingly enough, anxiety failed to grip me this time around. The truth is—I may never unravel what led my father down this path entirely; peculiarly enough—my knowledge about him extended only as far as my observations and the stories I had been told. With my hands tightly clasped together, I mustered the courage to look directly at my father.

"Dad, why do you indulge in these self-destructive habits?"

Exhaling a plume of smoke into the air—keeping it at a distance from me—my father averted his gaze momentarily before locking eyes with me. He took a significant pause of approximately ten seconds before offering his response—not that I was in any rush to receive an answer; I simply desired to understand if there was something I could do to change his circumstances and restore happiness within our family.

"I don't know..." he mumbled hesitantly, casting his eyes downward towards his feet. "I suppose it all began with an overwhelming sense of loneliness from the very beginning.

I needed something to keep me company...you see...ever since...my family fell apart...my troubled past led me down this path...and once started, breaking free became impossible. It's like an escape for me..."

At that moment, a flood of thoughts overwhelmed me—weren't we already a family? You, mom, Reynold, and myself? You have built the wonderful family you always desired. We reside in a three-story house and have all the necessities for survival and happiness. So why did you feel compelled to jeopardize our family's bliss? Why did you allow the darkness of your past to seize control over your life? Why, oh why?"

I sat there in silence, resisting the urge to shout at my father. My mind was filled with questions, but I chose to keep them to myself. Emotions surged through me, yet I refused to let them show. So there I sat, a 12-year-old without a voice in front of my father. No regrets, just a lack of confidence to stand up and protest.

Almost every night was difficult because the house echoed with the sounds of family warfare. Anxiety would grip me as my father called us to the dinner table, ready to ignite a new argument about something trivial. It felt like living in a never-ending nightmare. He always seemed bothered by every little thing, blaming us for draining his finances and deeming us useless tools. Each time he made it worse than before. It's frustrating, you know? Especially when you genuinely love your parents and care about them. They fight over the smallest things and escalate it into something big. But when they start yelling and throwing things at each other, my brother and I are powerless to stop it. We're mere spectators in their battles. And it doesn't end there; verbal abuse leads to physical abuse that comes dangerously close to fatal encounters, followed by emotional torment. Yet we endure it all somehow.

I never wanted this for my family. All I wanted was happiness and love between my parents without the constant fighting. A peaceful family life was my dream. Night after night, I cried myself to sleep hoping this reality would fade away like a bad dream, but it persisted every day because dreams don't repeat themselves like that. So, I had no choice but to accept that my parents would never find love for each other and our family would never be truly happy.

IV

Questioning Dad's Self Destruction Habits

Eventually, my mother decided to return to work to provide better financial support for our family. With her 10 years of experience as a travel agent, she landed a position as the head of immigration at one of the top companies in Bangalore. Her office was located 25 miles away from our home. She would leave early in the morning and return at 10 p.m. every night. My father's job allowed him to stay home or travel when required. Since my mom was working full-time, my father took charge of cooking whenever he was home. He had remarkable culinary skills and could whip up the most delicious meals for our table. My mother was an excellent cook as well, so it's safe to say that both my parents were equally talented in the kitchen. This explains why I gained weight during middle school; their cooking was simply irresistible.

When it comes to my school days, I was just an ordinary student. Sure, I had good grades, but there was always a sense of competition among my peers. Looking back, elementary school was pretty average. I excelled academically and had no trouble making friends. However, as middle school approached, something changed - my eating habits. I didn't realize that food could contribute to weight gain, so I started eating more without much thought. In my naive mind, I believed that laziness caused people to become overweight rather than the actual culprit - food itself. This lack of understanding led me down the path of developing an eating disorder and experiencing significant weight gain.

Returning to middle school after summer break was challenging for me. It was during this time that my science teacher confronted me about my weight gain. I felt at a loss for words because I couldn't explain why my body was changing so drastically. Eventually, through research and self-discovery, I learned about the natural process of puberty and how it affects the body's development. Despite this newfound knowledge, it didn't alleviate the emotional struggles that came with being overweight.

In an attempt to cope with these emotions, emotional eating became a regular part of my routine once again. It became difficult for me to determine whether my sadness stemmed from being overweight or from society's perception of attractiveness.

However difficult those times were for me at school, there were precious moments spent with my father in the evenings that brought joy into my life. Watching comedy movies together in his room became our favourite pastime activity; we would laugh endlessly even after watching the same movie multiple times over. These moments held immense value because they were instances where true happiness radiated between father and daughter.

After each movie ended, deep conversations between us would ensue - conversations centred around morals, cultural diversity, philosophy, and maintaining a positive outlook on life itself. He instilled within me a drive to work hard and pursue my dreams relentlessly.

They say that alcohol can bring out the worst in people, and unfortunately, my father fell victim to this truth. Behind his struggles with alcoholism was a charismatic personality that everyone adored. He was an exceptional father to both me and my brother, as well as a devoted husband to my mother. However, his refusal to address his bad habits hindered him from reaching his full potential. The stubbornness within him prevented any desire for personal growth.

I had an incredibly close bond with my father; I proudly referred to myself as "Daddy's Girl." The little moments we shared, filled with laughter and small gestures of affection, were priceless to me. In those moments, he treated me like royalty.

On the other hand, the relationship between my brother and father was far from amicable. To say there was tension between them would be an understatement - it was more like constant conflict. I never fully understood why they clashed so intensely; I chose not to interfere or delve into their issues. During our teenage years, my brother Reynold became extremely introverted which added another layer of complexity to our family dynamics. Despite our constant fights and rivalry, deep down we all loved each other immensely. It taught me that sometimes people express their love through hate - it's their way of showing how much they truly care about you. So, when your sibling says they hate you, take it with a grain of salt because love can be expressed in strange ways.

My father had a unique profession as a fashion designer. He would frequently travel for work, leaving him absent from our daily lives. However, this allowed him the incredible opportunity to explore different parts of the world and immerse himself in various cultures. His experiences were not only eye-opening but also educational for me. Whenever he returned, he would bring back designer clothes and chocolates from the places he visited, which fascinated me greatly. These items became cherished keepsakes that represented my father's creativity.

Occasionally, our entire family would surprise him with a visit to his current location. Although it was meant to be a joyous occasion for bonding and creating beautiful memories together, my father's behaviour often marred these vacations. Instead of cherishing quality time with his loved ones, he would become abusive and ruin the atmosphere. I don't have any pleasant memories of peaceful family holidays due to his volatile actions.

Interestingly, when my father wasn't around, there was a sense of peace within our family unit. We missed his presence but were relieved from the turmoil caused by his abusive behaviour. It was during those moments that I truly cherished being with my mother, brother, and grandmother in an environment free from violence.

Despite having all the materialistic possessions that a girl my age could desire, there was one thing missing: a genuine family connection. Alcohol had taken control of my father's life, transforming him into someone unrecognizable and morally compromised. His mood swings ranged from extreme enthusiasm to intense rage within short periods, causing immense anxiety for me.

There were instances when I stumbled upon hidden alcohol bottles under beds or inside drawers and wardrobes. My mother even suspected my father of drug abuse after finding traces of substances concealed in drawers. When confronted about it, he denied consuming drugs but claimed they were prescribed medications—an explanation too complex for me to understand at such a young age.

ℵ

One evening stands out vividly in my memory. After taking a shower, I couldn't find my hairdryer and asked my father for help. He instructed me to sit in front of the dressing mirror, and to my surprise, I heard the familiar sound of a hairdryer. Emotions overwhelmed me, and tears welled up in my eyes for reasons I couldn't fully comprehend. At twelve years old, there was my father drying my hair while I sat on the drawer chair by the dressing mirror. Unexplainable tears glistened in his eyes, conveying a depth of emotion that left me speechless. It was an incredibly poignant moment—one that tugged at the heartstrings of our father-daughter bond. With utmost care and gentleness, he lovingly combed through every strand of my hair without causing any discomfort.

It's moments like these that tug at a parent's heartstrings. They know that one day their children will grow up and leave the nest. There's this deep-rooted feeling inside them, knowing that they can never relive those precious moments of taking care of their kids during their childhood. It's truly something special. Every parent shares this unique bond with their child, and they would go to great lengths to make those moments last. Absolutely anything!

The clock had already struck half past nine, and I felt the need for some fresh air. I made my way to my bedroom window, gazing out at the night sky adorned with shimmering stars. Lost in the beauty of the dark expanse above me, I suddenly noticed a figure standing beside me, arms crossed. It was my father. While my mother was still on her way home from work, there he stood next to me, his usual self not entirely sober but coherent enough to walk and talk. I often wonder how much his body can endure despite indulging in alcoholism, smoking, and drugs; it seems invincible.

"Dad, do you love mom?" I blurted out while continuing to gaze at the starry sky, attempting to mentally count each shimmering speckle of. light. To say I wasn't apprehensive would be an understatement; I was anxiously awaiting his response.

"Yes, sweetheart, I do," he replied softly as he looked down at me with tenderness in his eyes.

A smile crept across my face; his gentle tone had a way of soothing my nerves.

"How much do you love her?" I turned to face my father directly and peered deep into his eyes in search of an answer. Slowly but surely, my nervousness started fading away as a newfound confidence washed over me like a cool breeze on a crisp evening.

"The kind of love that makes me willing to sacrifice my life for her happiness, that's how much I love her."

"Dad, if you truly care about Mom's happiness, why can't you work on it?" I inquired.

"What do you mean?" he asked, furrowing his brow in confusion.

"Daddy, can't you do something to make Mom happy?" I asked earnestly.

"Do you have any suggestions?" he responded spontaneously, crossing his arms.

"Can you overcome alcoholism?" I wanted to test the limits of my father's love for my mother. I questioned whether his commitment to her was genuine or just a passing curiosity. With numerous doubts swirling in my mind, I kept my hopes alive, secretly wishing upon a shooting star that streaked across the night sky.

My father glanced down at me, sporting a smile that masked his inner turmoil. After a brief moment of silence, he mustered up an answer.

"Sweetheart, I'm puzzled as to why we're having this conversation when it comes to how my alcoholism affects the love between your mother and me."

"Do you even realize what you're doing to yourself, Dad? Have you taken a good look at the person you've become under the influence of alcohol? It has tainted your true essence. Not even counselling seems capable of resolving this issue. Can't you see? It's tearing us apart. It's driving us insane because the individual alcohol has turned you into is far from desirable... and yet, Dad, you are so much more than that. You're intelligent, compassionate, and possess an irresistible charm... I know this because you're my father... And if you don't take action soon... we might lose everything... So I implore you to change and become an example of transformation... If you can change, then be the change that inspires others... Think of it as gaining something rather than losing something by making this choice... You understand what is at stake and what choices lie before us..."

My father was left utterly speechless, grappling for the right words to either validate or refute my recent statement. To my surprise, he abruptly stormed out of the room, forcefully shutting the door behind him. In an instant, tears began cascading down my cheeks as I sank to the floor in despair.

V

Making A Deal With Dad

"Hey," a voice startled me from my thoughts. "Can we talk?"

I turned to face my father, noticing the seriousness etched on his face. My body trembled, feeling weak under the weight of stress. I was too overwhelmed to even muster a smile, so I remained silent and allowed him to lead the conversation.

"I've thought long and hard about what you said... and I need to take action..."

I crossed my arms and listened intently as my father continued. "I know I haven't been the best husband to your mother or the best father to you and your brother... But losing you is something I cannot bear... We may have our fair share of chaos as a family... There will be moments when we despise each other, when we entertain thoughts of tearing each other apart... but that doesn't mean it's the end of the world... We'll get through this by providing moral support for one another... We'll learn to love unconditionally because that's what being a family is all about..."

Just as I thought his words would bring clarity, doubts crept back in. "What about your habits, Dad? Don't you want to change?"

"If only it were that simple... but I'm willing to work on it in exchange for something..."

As I delved into the matter at hand, a wave of curiosity washed over me. The request from my father both intrigued and unsettled me, as it carried a sense of empowerment and nervousness simultaneously. I was willing to do whatever it took to mend the bond with my father.

"So, what is it that you desire in return, Dad?" I asked cautiously.

My father's eyes welled up with tears as he approached me.

"I want you to make me proud... I want you to excel in your studies, especially in math... and if your determination drives you to give your utmost effort, I will be more than willing to accommodate your wishes for the sake of our family."

When it came to academics, I was neither an average student nor an exceptionally brilliant one. My performance teetered between the two extremes. However, very few people were aware of my hidden intellectual capabilities, as they often underestimated me. Both my parents and teachers held high expectations for my academic achievements, but I never took them seriously. Truth be told, studying didn't particularly interest me. While I enjoyed learning new things, the concept of exams didn't sit well with me. Sometimes my mind would wander off or fail to retain the information I studied. Exams seemed to define my intellectual worth and that always left me feeling remorseful.

In exchange for our family's happiness, my father sought a favour from me. Part of me doubted his sincerity in wanting to change himself for our sake but his burning desire for my academic success became evident through his words and actions. With a glimmer of hope in my heart, I decided to give myself a chance. I promised my father that I wouldn't disappoint him and that giving up was not an option.

Okay then! Can we talk about math for a moment? Personally speaking (no offence intended towards mathematicians), numbers have never been my cup of tea – especially when it comes to algebra. Geometry, on the other hand, holds a special place in my heart. I've always been captivated by questions about shapes and sizes. The compass and pencil were my trusty companions during those lessons. Exploring the concepts of diameter and radius in a circle was particularly fascinating to me. Of course, I understand the basics, but I wouldn't consider myself an expert by any means. I can handle addition, multiplication, subtraction, division, fractions, and common divisors quite well. Solving problems related to shapes brings me joy. However, when it comes to formulas and equations... let's just say they make me squirm a bit!

If I had the power to eliminate one subject from my life, it would undoubtedly be algebra. I fail to see the practicality of using formulas and equations in real-life situations. Why must we waste our time learning something that will be utterly useless in the future? Maybe it has some relevance for certain careers, but seriously? Why do we have to endure this torment?

My father, like any brilliant mathematician, was a master of numbers. He never relied on a calculator; his brain was his calculator. I always marvelled at how his mind could function with such precision. He claimed it was a gift, but to gifted individuals like him, it seemed more like mental torture.

Yet there was something deep within me that pushed me forward. Something that motivated me to excel. My father had never asked anything of me before, but now he needed my help. I couldn't let him down; I had to make him proud.

"Challenge accepted," I declared as I shook hands with my father. Meanwhile, my mother had been called away to Chennai for work purposes. The thought of her being so far from me haunted me every second of my day. I tried distracting myself with various activities, but it was difficult to focus knowing she wouldn't be there.

"It's just two days, baby, don't cry," she reassured me for the tenth time as she enveloped me in a warm embrace.

To me, it wasn't just a matter of two days; it was the swirling thoughts and confusion in my mind that bothered me most. They collided and clashed within me, creating an overwhelming sense of chaos. Trying to shake them off and keep myself composed proved futile; they overwhelmed every attempt at self-control. So I surrendered and collapsed onto my bed while watching my mother pack her suitcase. My brother stepped in and offered her assistance with carrying it as well. With tears still stinging in my eyes, I weakly waved goodbye to my mother. She kissed my forehead and promised me that Dad would take care of us. Deep down, a part of me knew it would be the opposite. I walked over to the window, pulling back the curtains to catch a final glimpse of my mother stepping into the taxi. As it drove away and disappeared, I let out a sigh and closed the window, drawing the curtains shut. Slowly, I made my way back to bed and plopped down on it. Staring at the ceiling, my mind drifted off into space.

Would I be able to survive without my mother for two days? Would she be there to protect me if my drunken father became violent? How could I possibly sleep soundly without her goodnight kisses? That night, it dawned on me just how much my mother meant to me. She was my entire world; every fibre of my being revolved around her presence. My father was also a part of that world, despite his alcohol-induced behaviour that often left me resentful towards him. But as a Christian, I had learned about forgiveness and letting go...of everything! It wasn't an easy journey, but with time, I managed to rebuild the trust I once had in him.

A little while later, I strolled into the guest room, my trusty laptop in tow. Boredom had consumed me, so I decided to log onto FACEBOOK, GMAIL, and other social media platforms in an attempt to alleviate it. Ah, those were the days when my addiction to social media was at its peak; being a part of that virtual world meant everything to me. It felt as though my entire existence revolved around it. It wasn't just the concept of "Social Media" that attracted me, but the vast expanse of the "Internet" itself. The internet served as my one-stop destination for entertainment and knowledge alike. I began to comprehend its numerous benefits and gradually developed an infatuation with this "New Media."

VI

A Night Of Horror

Before immersing myself in the realm of cyberspace, I held a deep connection with Indian Cinema. Growing up in India made me a proud and avid fan of Bollywood - a vibrant tapestry of various genres that never failed to astound me. I would often daydream about being a part of this enchanting world; however, deep down inside, I knew it was nothing more than a whimsical figment of my imagination. My parents understood this and believed that such a life was not what I truly desired for myself. Nevertheless, my dreams persisted.

As I entered the guest room with anticipation swirling within me, the aroma wafting from the kitchen caught my attention - unmistakably chicken! My mouth began to water at the mere scent permeating through the air.

Soon enough, dinner was ready and my father called out for me to join him at the table. His culinary skills were always impeccable, and every dish he prepared delighted my taste buds immensely - particularly his non-vegetarian creations. After savouring every bite during our mealtime together, I promptly returned to my laptop once again.

However, not long after resuming my digital escapades, my father approached me and instructed me to shut down the laptop and head to bed. An overwhelming sense of fear washed over me as I complied with his request - my mother was not around, further intensifying my apprehension. As I pressed the SHUT DOWN button, an unusual delay occurred before the laptop finally powered off. It struck me as odd since laptops typically shut down much more swiftly. That night, with my father's presence looming over me, nervousness consumed every fibre of my being. Beads of sweat formed on my forehead, and I trembled uncontrollably. At that moment, I resigned myself to the belief that everything was about to crumble.

My father glanced at the laptop and posed a question that sent shivers down my spine: "What have you done to this laptop, Rene?" Petrified, I stood frozen like a statue, fixated on that dreaded device which seemed determined to torment me. Goodness gracious! I knew for certain that trouble awaited me.

"Dad, I swear I didn't do anything! I can't fathom why it's taking so long to shut down," I softly responded in an attempt to defend myself.

Dad instructed me to call my brother for assistance. Dialling his number quickly connected us as he answered from his room. My brother took one look at the laptop before informing us that there might be some technical issue causing the delay in shutting down. With bated breaths and anticipation hanging heavy in the air, we sat in silence while hoping for the laptop's eventual compliance. Meanwhile, Dad gazed at us with eyes brimming with anger. My brother knew all too well that Dad might unleash his fury upon either myself or our grandmother; hence he patiently waited for the laptop to comply so that he could guide me safely off to bed. Oh, how grateful I was for having such a protective brother by my side - it reassured me that I was safe!

Despite our best efforts, my father lost control of himself as per usual, exacerbating an already tense situation. Impatience got the better of him, and he placed the blame squarely on my shoulders for whatever misdeeds he believed I had committed against the laptop. He sternly warned me to never lay a finger on it again, and I nodded in agreement, too terrified to do otherwise. In his rage, he even attempted to strike me; however, my brother swiftly intervened and pushed Dad away. The scene unfolded before my eyes - my heart pounding in sheer terror. What on earth was I going to do now?

I knew deep down that my brother possessed the strength to restrain our father effectively since Dad was weakened by alcohol and lacked his usual faculties. With a firm grip on Dad's arm, my brother turned to me with urgency in his eyes and said, "Sis, lock yourself and granny in the room. Don't open it until I give you the signal." Following his instructions dutifully, I secured the door behind us and immediately reached out to our mother for help. Through tearful sobs, I recounted every detail of the distressing situation.

Locked away with my grandmother by my side, we awaited further developments with trepidation.

My brother, in an act of defiance, attempted to physically remove our father from the situation. He engaged in a struggle with him, forcefully throwing him onto his bed. Afterwards, my brother locked the main door and hurriedly joined us. Urgently, he instructed us to open our room door. Without hesitation, I complied while my mother remained on the phone with me. I felt relieved having both my mother and brother by my side. My mother continued her conversation with me as my brother stood beside me. Their presence alleviated all my fears and worries. I expressed gratitude towards my brother for protecting me and being there for me during this ordeal. I am truly thankful to have such a supportive sibling in my life.

Upon hearing my brother's voice, Mom insisted on seeing if he was alright. She engaged in a heartfelt conversation with him as he poured out his pain and suffering to her. It was a sombre moment witnessing my usually stoic brother cry in anguish and distress. Tears streamed down his cheeks as his eyes reddened from the intensity of his emotions. It is uncommon for boys to openly display their vulnerability through tears, but my brother's pain transcended societal expectations that day. This experience deeply affected me as well; it pierced straight into the core of my heart, allowing me to empathize with his anguish on a profound level.

Overwhelmed by everything that had transpired, I opened the window hoping that fresh air would cleanse away all that had occurred before me. I succumbed to tears and questioned why these events had unfolded.

In search of answers, I entered my brother's room only to find the overturned television set and three drops of blood on the floor - faintly crimson! My gaze shifted between those drops of blood and Shane; shock evident on my face as I questioned him urgently, "Bro... are you okay? Whose blood is this? Are you hurt? Did dad-"

"It's Dad's blood!" he interjected; his gaze downcast. At that moment, my heart shattered into countless pieces and ceased beating for a fleeting second.

My brother later clarified that our father was physically unharmed due to his actions. The bloodshed was a result of an old injury resurfacing, causing the bandage to come undone and the wound to bleed. I longed to be with my father, to tend to his wounds and offer him solace. This realization only intensified my sorrow as I wept uncontrollably. I could feel the weight of his pain in my own heart. But why did it have to escalate this way? Why did our father resort to violence? A simple reprimand would have sufficed; why did he choose physical harm instead? Was I truly deserving of such treatment? Had I committed some grievous offence warranting a slap or a brutal assault?

Throughout it all, my brother consistently prioritized my well-being over his own. He constantly checked on me, making sure I was alright and had everything I needed. Even in the darkest hours of the night, he offered me his shoulder to cry on, and without hesitation, I accepted his comforting presence. Like always, he remained my protector and guardian; for that unwavering love and care, I am eternally grateful. Thank you once again, Jesus, for blessing me with an extraordinary brother who loves me unconditionally.

ꕥ

The following day arrived, and Grandmother rose early to approach the main entrance. As usual, Father remained inebriated from the previous night's indulgence in alcohol. Father beseeched Grandmother to open the door as he was bleeding profusely and required assistance to staunch the flow. With compassion, Grandmother complied and unlatched the door. She held onto hope that my father would exhibit normalcy, but her assumption proved erroneous. She believed he would not pose a threat to us, yet she was mistaken. Opening the door allowed Father entry into our abode. Shortly thereafter, one of our tenants arrived to deliver the rent payment. Grandmother accepted the funds on behalf of our mother, fully aware of the potential consequences should the father gain possession of the money. Thus, she endeavoured to keep it out of his reach.

Five minutes later, I heard sounds of someone weeping and expressing agony— that "someone" was my grandmother. Startled awake by these distressing noises, I witnessed Father berating her with hostile fervour. He menaced her with a chilling tone: "Aunty, hand over the rent money or face dire consequences..." Father coveted money for his insatiable habit of smoking 40 cigarettes daily and consuming copious amounts of alcohol—his sole liquid sustenance—which only intensified his torment inflicted upon us. However, grandmother steadfastly refused to surrender the funds to him. He even attempted physical aggression by gesturing menacingly with raised bloodshot eyes and an uplifted hand poised for violence against her.

Before I could voice my objection or intervene in any way, my brother came swiftly to our rescue. Our rooms were situated adjacent to each other but separate entities unto themselves. Grabbing hold of Father's wrist firmly yet deftly twisting it away from harm's reach, my brother forcefully propelled him backwards onto his bed ensured that our main entrance was securely locked, and promptly made his way to our side. My brother possessed inherent strength, capable of lifting and discarding any object with ease. Did I mention that he frequented the gym to cultivate such physical prowess? Well, he did. I stood in awe of his actions and immediately checked on his grandmother's well-being. Once father was out of her line of sight, she regained composure though tears flowed freely from both our eyes.

I promptly dialled my mother's number and recounted the morning's events in detail. She reassured me not to fret as she would be returning home later that afternoon.

VII

Mom Returns

Around 12:30 PM, Mother arrived at our doorstep, finally granting me a sense of relief.

Inwardly, I wanted to shout triumphantly, "Now that my mother has returned, nothing in this world can touch or harm me." Whenever my mother was present, I felt an unwavering sense of security, empowered to pursue my desires without restraint or hindrance.

No one could impede me when she was by my side. My love for her knew no bounds; indeed, I would sacrifice anything for her. Upon reaching home, Mother rushed towards us. Overwhelmed with emotions, I burst into tears and embraced her tightly, finding solace in the embrace of her arms. Both my brother and grandmother joined this precious reunion. Suddenly and unexpectedly, Father overheard our gathering and approached us with a softened gaze upon sighting Mother.

Father took a seat on the sofa as directed by Mom, who demanded an explanation for his problematic behaviour and questioned why he sought to inflict harm upon his children. Mother always believed father fell short as a husband but acknowledged his flawed nature as a father during tumultuous times. I harboured disdain towards him due to his deplorable tactics and demeanour—his erratic nature proved unbearable. The moment he nearly laid a hand on me became the final straw in our strained relationship. Forgiveness may come one day, but that day is not imminent.

It's unfortunate how much we can't stand his torments anymore. The way he physically assaulted my mother, it's truly heartbreaking. Sadly, I felt guilty for telling the truth. And what's even sadder is that they haven't even finalized their divorce yet!

You see, my dad wanted a divorce. My mom believed it was for the best. Eventually, my mom decided to meet with a lawyer. I accompanied her to the meeting place where we were supposed to discuss everything with the lawyer. My mom poured her heart out, sharing all the details about her life with my dad. It was disheartening because I didn't want them to split up. They loved each other, they were married, they had built a life together and had us kids. I didn't want it all to end. However, at such a young age, I couldn't fully grasp what was happening or know what to do about it as a thirteen-year-old.

I always found it strange when my dad wasn't himself anymore. Deep down, I knew that my parents would eventually separate and that our family would never be the picture-perfect fairy tale we always hoped for.

Perhaps the more important question is why people get married in the first place if they ultimately end up divorcing. Usually, those who find themselves in court trying to resolve their failed marriage are primarily concerned with practical matters and just want things sorted out quickly and efficiently. They seek an agreement that can bring order to their situation—a comprehensive agreement covering all aspects involved in divorce proceedings—such as child custody and visitation rights—a situation where two conflicting spouses often struggle to differentiate between their roles as husband/wife and parents.

It seems like these struggles stem from power dynamics and control issues between separating couples when it comes down to defining parental responsibilities over children—power struggles and control battles become significant factors in these circumstances—and this can indeed be quite disheartening.

I've witnessed this scenario countless times, and it always seems to follow a similar pattern. The king and queen are supposed to be deeply in love, supporting each other while raising their precious little Princess. A Princess adorned in fluffy pink gowns with tiaras shimmering in her perfectly styled hair. But I suppose this is a different kind of fairy tale. Mommy and Daddy are just a different kind of King and Queen, and I am a different kind of Princess. Everything about our situation is unique, life has turned out differently for us.

ꕥ

That night, I had a vivid dream that left me feeling unsettled. As I reluctantly rose from my bed, I braced myself to confront my mother about something that was bothering her. However, when I found her in the living room, she was hiding her face in her hands and sobbing uncontrollably.

"Mum?" My voice trembled as I held onto the bannister for support. The anger I had felt earlier dissipated instantly, replaced by concern. "What's wrong?"

"It's your father," she managed to say between sobs.

"Why?" I asked, my heart sinking.

"He's never been this late before...and when I called him...he didn't answer," she said with a shaky voice.

"Mom," I sighed in exasperation, "You know how Dad is. He's always caught up with work. Maybe he's just working overtime."

I sat down beside her on our cosy red couch - it could easily fit four people comfortably - and placed a reassuring hand on her shoulder.

But Mom seemed unconvinced and bit her lip anxiously. "No," she insisted stubbornly, "I don't think so..."

"Seriously?" I shook my head at her disbelievingly. "What do you think he could be doing?"

Before Mom could respond, the door suddenly swung open and there stood Dad... visibly drunk! Tears welled up in my eyes at the sight of him.

VIII

Mom Discovers A Second Chance At Love

Life had dealt her a tough hand. After years of being tormented by her husband, she had almost given up hope of finding love again. But fate had other plans in store for her. In the most serendipitous way, she crossed paths with a kind-hearted stranger who would change her life forever. Their initial meeting was like something out of a Hollywood movie - sparks flew and time seemed to stand still. It was as if the universe conspired to bring them together. Their chemistry was undeniable, and they quickly discovered that they shared many common interests and values. As their relationship blossomed, they faced numerous obstacles along the way. Life threw curveballs their way, testing their commitment to each other. But through it all, their love only grew stronger. Their story is one of resilience and perseverance in the face of adversity. It serves as a reminder that it's never too late to find happiness and fulfillment in life. So grab some tissues and prepare yourself for an emotional rollercoaster ride as you delve into this captivating tale of love rediscovered. You won't be able to put it down until you've reached the heartwarming conclusion that will leave you believing in second chances.

It was January 14th of 2007 when Mom informed us that one of her acquaintances would be paying us a visit – specifically a male friend. A white Baleno car pulled up outside our home and Mom arrived with him by her side. They entered the house together while Mom went off to fetch something for him; he settled down on the swing in our balcony. Sensing my reserved nature and hesitancy to engage in conversation, Mom encouraged me to strike up a dialogue with him. I was typically labeled as "mute" or "speechless" rather than someone who actively participated in conversations. With a hint of shyness, I approached him and exchanged pleasantries. He inquired about my school and various other things, to which I dutifully responded. His constant laughter during our conversation started to irritate me and made me slightly uncomfortable. Later that evening, we all sat down for dinner, and after a couple of hours, I drifted into a deep sleep.

In the past, whenever Dad was present and Mom brought someone home, he would often get intoxicated at night and end up physically abusing us after the guest had left. However, on that particular day, Dad was away working abroad and had no knowledge of the situation at home.

Whenever he worked overseas, he rarely kept in touch with us – sometimes going weeks or even months without calling. Mom informed me that her friend would be staying overnight with us.

During the night's slumber, I abruptly woke up in search of my mother's comforting presence beside me, but she was nowhere to be found. Panic struck through my heart as she was supposed to sleep by my side. Frantically searching everywhere in the house yielded no results; she had vanished without a trace. It crossed my mind that she might have gone out somewhere. As it turned out, Mom had left with her male friend for a late-night drive (I learned this from her explanation the following day). During their outing, they shared their life stories – including Mom's experiences with her husband – which created an emotional bond between them.

From time to time when Mom received messages from her friend on her phone, she would excitedly show them to my aunt or close friends but never directly shared them with me. It made me wonder why she kept those messages a secret from me. Gradually, I started noticing changes in Mom's behavior – she spent more time on her phone, her friend would drop her home after work, and other subtle alterations. It was evident that love had entered her life, and the transformation was noticeable to anyone who paid attention.

When a woman falls in love, every little aspect of her changes and it becomes noticeable to anyone around her. However, I couldn't understand why my mom was behaving this way. Was it out of a desire for revenge? That didn't seem likely. Why would she want to seek revenge? Perhaps what she really needed was someone to love and spend her life with. But then, why couldn't my dad fulfill that role? These thoughts swirled in my mind as I sat under the dark sky, questioning everything.

One night, while sleeping beside my mom in her room, I mustered up the courage to express my feelings. "Mom," I said, "you have every right to be with the man you love and you don't need my permission for that. But sometimes I wish I had known about both of you." Mom kissed me tenderly and whispered a heartfelt "Thank you." Whenever I spoke to her, there was always an open honesty between us. She was not just a mother but also my best friend - someone whom I could confide in without fear or reservation.

Gradually, this secret affair between mom and her male friend blossomed into something more significant. Mom had finally found solace in a relationship with this person she had introduced earlier. It became apparent that she sought refuge from the unhappiness caused by dad's behavior and struggles with alcoholism. This affair unfolded during one of dad's work trips abroad.

One fateful day, when mom informed dad that one of her friends would be visiting our home, it became clear who she was referring to – the guy she had been seeing secretly all along. Whenever dad was within earshot distance from us, I playfully teased mom about their connection using subtle hints and innuendos. Dad remained oblivious; he assumed this person was simply another friend after a brief introduction from mom.

At some point, my father discovered that mom was involved with another man. He even went as far as reading the messages on her phone while she was preoccupied with something else. This revelation only fueled his anger and made him resort to drinking even more heavily. That same night, in a drunken state, dad confronted mom, my brother, and me about the affair. The situation escalated quickly, but none of us dared to answer his questions. This only enraged him further.

If we refused to comply with his demands or answer his inquiries honestly, he would resort to violence – threatening to harm or even kill us until we confessed the truth. My brother stood ready for a physical altercation if necessary, and mom displayed resilience and strength; she was prepared to fight for herself and her children. We tried our best to endure this volatile situation, but it became unbearable. Whenever dad attempted to harm us physically, my brother would step in and restrain him before carrying him back to his room. If not for these interventions, who knows what he might have done? I often pondered why my own father wanted to destroy our family's happiness.

Eventually, after being thrown back into his room by my brother once again during one of these episodes, dad attempted to get up and continue the fight against us. In response, we swiftly shut the door as a protective measure. Enraged by this obstacle, he resorted to breaking the window glasses in an attempt to gain entry through that route instead. The shattering glass echoed throughout the house as shards scattered across the floor – leaving us bewildered about what our next move should be.

It was at this critical moment that we decided it was necessary to call the police for help; they arrived within ten minutes of our distress call. Our neighbors also overheard the commotion unfolding within our home - they were frightened by the chaos and began suspecting that my dad had gone insane or become unhinged somehow. However, he wasn't truly insane; he was merely intoxicated and had lost control of his senses.

My father, in a drunken state, insisted on fabricating lies to the police as a means of saving himself from the consequences of his actions. However, due to his intoxication, they were unable to incarcerate him. Eventually, we managed to convey our situation to the police, and I even requested that he be punished for his actions. This plea resonated with the authorities, and they decided not to imprison him. Instead, they took him to the police station as a warning against further harm towards our family. It was during this time that my father came to realize the gravity of his mistake.

We chose to forgive him out of necessity. Hatred had no place in our home or our lives. If we held onto anger, it would only fester within us and consume us slowly. Therefore, forgiveness became our only option. Despite the pain he caused us and his occasional excessive drinking, there were also moments of love and special gestures that compensated for his shortcomings. It was evident that he loved us deeply, even though those words were seldom spoken aloud. Over time, we came to understand that genuine love could never inflict harm upon others.

There was another reason why we chose forgiveness - something my father had once said in a drunken state long ago. In those moments of madness reflected in his eyes, we knew it would pass; however, there was always a fear that one day it might not fade away completely. He confessed through slurred speech and struggled with words but managed to express himself: "This is nothing compared to what my parents used to do to me!" Even though these words were muttered quietly, they struck a deep chord within us.

We forgave him because he couldn't forgive himself; anger had consumed him entirely and transformed him into someone unrecognizable. Anger is an insidious poison - it devours its host rapidly and has far-reaching consequences. We learned not to judge him during those moments but rather during the times when he forgot his anger and sought forgiveness. It was in those fleeting instants that we saw his true intentions - to bring happiness to our lives. And so, we always forgave him.

ꟹ

That same night, we gathered as a family to discuss our next steps, contemplating leaving the house behind. My mother, grandmother, brother, and I packed our suitcases and retired for the night. A while later, my mother received a call from the police inquiring if she was ready to leave my father. She informed them that she would do so after an hour.

The following morning, we all sat on the sofa deep in thought and conversation. Suddenly, my father overheard us talking and implored us to open the door. My mother complied with his request and he entered silently before finally speaking up: "I apologize for what happened yesterday. I lost control." His hands were clasped together as he uttered these words - a clear indication of his sincerity.

My mother declared that she no longer wanted to live with him; she expressed her intention of moving out with us children. It was then my turn to address him directly. Despite his desperate pleas for another chance, we had already given him ample opportunities.

Taking a deep breath, I sorrowfully told him: "Dad, enough is enough. We cannot endure any more of this turmoil; our lives have been filled with nightmares for far too long. If we continue living like this, who knows what may become of us? Look at the shattered glass from your outburst." These words struck me like a hammer blow - my world felt shattered into pieces; my body went numb as tears threatened to spill forth uncontrollably. Deep down though, I knew that those words were not entirely genuine; they were spoken out of necessity at that moment in order for my father to acknowledge his mistake.

Living with him again became an impossible prospect for us, as there was always the fear that he might harm us or break his promises.

"I'm really sorry, sweetheart. I'll clean it up, but please, please, please give me another chance," he pleaded, folding his hands together.

"What do you want now, Dad?" my brother exclaimed with frustration.

"Son, I'm sorry," he said in a shaky voice that made my lips quiver.

"I know you won't forgive me. I've never been a good father, but everything I did was for your own sake. I'm sorry..." Dad's words hung in the air as my brother looked away, torn inside about whether to give him another chance or not. The weight of the unspoken words pressed on him.

My heart cried out so loudly, yet no one seemed to hear it. The pain was unbearable; breathing became almost impossible. I longed to forgive him and give him another chance. I wanted him to be my father and never be apart from him again. Memories flooded my mind - watching Munnabhai together and laughing uncontrollably, singing along while he played the guitar, his guidance on the right path in life - all turned into bittersweet memories that couldn't be erased. But sitting there with a numb body, unable to forgive myself for what I said, made it seem impossible to mend what was broken.

Finally gathering her courage, Mom spoke up: "We're leaving this house; I've endured enough from you over the past 18 years. To keep myself and my children safe, we're leaving you!" Dad didn't utter a word; yet deep inside his heart echoed cries of sorrow that only those closest could perceive. His mind was filled with thoughts left unspoken; he didn't know what else to say. He walked away and cleared away all the shattered glass pieces with an air of resignation. Part of me wanted to go after him but my body remained motionless on the spot. Memories overwhelmed me - bloodlust and all my losses. I felt like I was losing my father, but deep down, a glimmer of hope remained. His sad face was etched in my mind, but... I couldn't quite fathom what lay ahead. I was too young to understand; there was nothing I could do. Self-hatred consumed me and everything else around me.

Suddenly, Dad returned. He wasn't sure what else to say, but he felt compelled to speak up. Breaking the heavy silence with a somber tone, he uttered, "I'm not responsible for your decision to leave this house. Do whatever you want." With those words hanging in the air, he retreated to his room with a heart heavy with sadness. He wasn't severely intoxicated this time; just slightly under the influence - manageable enough.

We had prepared everything - our clothes, accessories, beddings, TV, and some utensils - ready for our departure. Mom called the moving company to transport all our belongings while Dad approached Mom once again and expressed that he wouldn't bear responsibility for us leaving. He even suggested that she draft a small agreement regarding our departure from the house - and she did so accordingly. We left the house and sought refuge at my aunt's place without bidding Dad goodbye since sadness consumed me in that moment; I simply followed Mom's lead. As we descended the stairs, Dad asked Mom for some money; she turned to Granny and said: "Give him some money for his drinks," and Granny obliged by handing him some cash.

My dad didn't ask for money to buy alcohol; he needed it because he was completely broke. However, despite what my mom had just told him, he stayed silent. He tried to speak, but no words came out. I looked at him, unaware that it would be the last time I saw him alive.

I took one final look at our house, marveling at its beauty. It was where I had spent my entire life and childhood. Leaving it meant leaving behind my friends, my crush, and all the memories we had made together. It was painful to say goodbye to such a place.

I closed my eyes and felt the wind gently rustling through my hair and tears.

"Please let this be a dream," I pleaded to the sky or anyone who could hear me. Opening my eyes, I wiped away my tears.

We relocated to our new residence, which now accommodates myself, my brother, my mother, and my grandmother. Our new home is a modest dwelling comprising two bathrooms, two bedrooms, a cozy living room, and a petite balcony. As part of our routine, our maid and grandmother would make regular visits to the house where our father resided in order to ensure his well-being.

IX

Worst Day Of My Life

On that eventful day, the 11th of December in 2009, a significant moment unfolded. It was when my dear grandmother graced my father's residence with her presence. In his customary kindness, he extended to her a steaming cup of coffee, which she gratefully accepted. The aroma and flavor of the coffee delighted her senses, bringing immense pleasure. Amidst their conversation, my father mentioned his impending journey to Delhi for urgent matters at hand. Inquiring about my well-being through our beloved granny, he conveyed an intense yearning to see me once more and expressed how deeply he missed having me in his life. Upon returning home, Granny shared these heartfelt sentiments with me, stirring within me an overwhelming sense of longing and affection that words alone cannot fully capture.

The bond between a daughter and her father runs deep,

unravelled by the profound love he holds for her—a love that surpasses his self-interest, where he is willing to make any sacrifice just to be by her side. As the evening wore on, my dad found solace in alcohol, while my grandmother had been present earlier. It was during this time that I stumbled upon his Facebook account on his laptop after his passing. In those moments, he began reflecting on his family, his children, and all those individuals with whom he had lost touch. The realization of how much we meant to him hit him hard as he acknowledged the grave mistakes he had made. He carried the burden of unforgiveness towards himself for these wrongdoings. It was at that very moment that he felt as though life held no purpose anymore. The loss of his beloved family—the very essence of what gave meaning to his existence—left him in a desolate state. Overwhelmed by it all, he tragically chose to end his own life by hanging himself from the ceiling fan. His feet no longer touched the chair; it lay abandoned on the floor as silence engulfed the room. There was no turning back now—he was gone forever. Everything had reached its ultimate conclusion. While Dad's suffering came to an end, it left behind a trail of anguish for everyone else left behind to bear.

In the final moments before succumbing to death, he gently shut his eyes, uttering my name in a faint whisper. His life slowly slipping away, he hung there suspended... It was a tragic act of self-inflicted demise, a poignant testament to the unbearable pain of living without his loved ones.

❧

I was enjoying my evening meal when suddenly I found

myself in a choking fit. It seemed that a piece of food had become lodged in my windpipe, causing me to choke. My mom heard my coughing and quickly came to my aid, providing me with water and comforting me by rubbing my back. Fortunately, I recovered soon after. According to popular belief, experiencing such a choking incident signifies that something negative has occurred or someone may be thinking ill of you. This made me wonder if everything was alright with my dad or if something unfortunate had happened to him. Naturally, I felt concerned and had trouble sleeping that night. My mind was filled with countless thoughts, preventing me from finding rest. The weight of these thoughts brought tears to my eyes as I reminisced about happier times.

The following day arrived, which happened to be December 12th. The maid arrived at the house where Dad resides but found his bedroom door closed shut. As she proceeded with her cleaning duties, she eventually discovered Dad hanging lifeless inside the room. She couldn't comprehend why he had taken such a drastic step without any warning signs indicating his intentions. Unbeknownst to her, Dad had tragically passed away. After finishing her tasks at Dad's place, the same maid came over to our house and informed us about his refusal to open the door of his room. We all grew increasingly worried upon hearing this news and many of us feared the worst—that he might have succumbed.

Later that evening, Granny decided it was necessary for her to personally investigate why Dad hadn't opened his bedroom door yet. Mom encouraged Granny's initiative and urged her to ascertain whether everything was fine with Dad or not while I remained at my aunt's residence under their care as both Mom and her fiancé went out.

Granny reached Dad's place swiftly and immediately entered his bedroom upon unlocking the door with trembling hands only to be confronted by the sight of Dad's lifeless body hanging motionless like a statue.

Overcome with shock and distress, she couldn't help but let out piercing screams for assistance. The sound of her cries reached the ears of our concerned neighbours who hurriedly rushed out from their homes to witness the devastating scene of Dad's lifeless form suspended in mid-air. Granny quickly dialled my aunt's number, her voice trembling as she informed her about Dad's tragic demise. Receiving this phone call was undoubtedly the most heart-wrenching moment of my entire existence. At that time, I happened to be with my aunt, and when she revealed the heartbreaking news that Dad had passed away, I was utterly stunned and found it incredibly difficult to accept this harsh reality. It felt as though something deep within me shattered into countless fragments—perhaps it was my heart itself. With tears streaming down my face, I gazed at a picture of God in front of me and succumbed to an overwhelming wave of sorrow, breaking down completely in that moment—a pain unlike any other I had ever experienced before.

A wife without her husband is commonly known as a 'widow.' But what do you call a child without a father? Is it a half-orphan or simply a fatherless child? To be honest, I don't have the answer and I don't want to know either. You see, I am now one of those children without a father, and just the sight of a father with his daughter brings back painful memories of him. He was truly the best father anyone could ever ask for. The day he left us was etched in my mind forever.

My aunt and I rushed to my dad's room in panic. As soon as she opened the door, she let out an ear-piercing scream and fainted on the spot. My brother came up behind me, tears streaming down his face as he stood there frozen in shock. The air seemed to escape from my lungs, making it difficult to breathe. There was no turning back. I watched as my dad swung back and forth on that rope, his lifeless body hanging before me. The fallen chair nearby added to the haunting scene. It felt like all hope had been sucked out of the room. My brother stood there motionless, unable to comprehend what had just happened, tears streaming down his face uncontrollably... It was such a dark phase that I found myself in - losing my dad forever in such a tragic way.

Seeing him hanging there with my yellowish-green skipping rope left me numb with disbelief. His angelic face flashed before my eyes, spinning my world into chaos. He had chosen that very rope to end it all... And silently, I blamed myself for leaving it there. But deep down, who knows? Even if I hadn't left that skipping rope behind, maybe he would have found another way. Granny called mom and delivered the devastating news that dad was gone. My aunt finally regained consciousness and broke down again at the sight of him. I couldn't control my tears, they just flowed endlessly. For a while, I kept quiet, unable to find the words to express my grief. Mom arrived within minutes and saw dad's lifeless body. We sat in complete silence for what felt like an eternity. When a home loses its soul, a heavy silence settles over the emptiness that will never be filled again. None of us had the strength to look at each other for comfort; silence filled every corner of the room. The atmosphere was heavy with sorrow and deep breaths were all we could hear.

X

Rest In Peace Dad

Mom picked up the phone and dialled 100, barely able to utter the words "My husband committed suicide."

The police finally arrived and witnessed the tragic scene of my dad hanging there. They instructed Mom to write a letter explaining his reasons for taking such drastic action and also informed one of Dad's relatives about what had happened. Later that evening, an ambulance came to take away Dad's lifeless body. I couldn't tear my eyes away from him, this man who was once called my 'father.' Memories of all the good times we shared flashed before me like a movie reel. I closed my eyes tightly as tears escaped from them. It felt like those precious moments would never return... they were gone forever.

They carefully lowered his lifeless body from the ropes and gently placed him on the stretcher. A white bed sheet was tenderly draped over him as he was taken away. Just like that, he was gone. The realization hit me like a wave of anger, an overwhelming urge to scream or break something. "I'll miss you, Daddy," I managed to whisper as I watched his body being carried into the ambulance. The commotion caught the attention of our nosy neighbours, which only added to my frustration. Rumours and false stories started circulating, but at that moment, I couldn't care less. What people didn't know were all those times I sat in my room with the volume turned up high on my TV, yet still heard my dad hurling abusive words at my mom.

They didn't know about the times he slapped me across the face while my mom dialled emergency services. They didn't know that he gave away my beloved dog just because I refused to cook him a meal. And they certainly didn't know about the time he emptied all of my hair products and lotions down the drain simply because I forgot to dust the bathroom floor – over 300 Rs worth of products wasted. In each of those moments, it was my mom who stood up for me, protecting me from him. She would cry and scream at him and call the police. He would be kicked out of our house and have to rely on a cab since he couldn't drive drunk (although driving under the influence seemed to pose no issue for him).

But after a few days – just a fleeting respite – her insecurities and vulnerabilities would consume her from within, drawing her back to him. And so, the cycle continued: his return followed by excessive drinking of Absolut Vodka; harm inflicted upon both my mother and me; his subsequent expulsion; then locking ourselves away while crying our hearts out. At 7:00, the service people took my dad's body to the hospital and requested his clothes. Later that evening, we returned to the house we were staying in, had a meal, and tried to sleep. The next day was supposed to be my dad's funeral. We woke up and got ready, heading back to the hospital where his body lay. Standing outside, we waited as time crawled by. Finally, after what felt like an eternity, they brought out his lifeless form. I took one last look at him – so handsome in his coat and trousers – knowing it would be my final memory of him dressed so elegantly. Tears streamed down my face. Life has a strange way of playing with us, doesn't it? When we crave life itself, it often denies us; yet when one relinquishes all desire for existence, it insists on survival.

The driver carefully transported his lifeless form into the waiting ambulance and we arrived at my house. A sombre ceremony was taking place outside, a farewell to my father's earthly vessel. We arrived just in time as a group of individuals reverently lifted his body and placed it in the coffin. The gathering grew, neighbours peering curiously into the casket, their eyes prying into an intimate moment that I wished to shield from their invasive gaze. Who did they think they were? I felt an overwhelming urge to shield my father's final moments from prying eyes. Helplessness washed over me, a feeling of despair settling deep within my heart. Suddenly, the priest arrived to offer his blessings upon my father's soul. Prayers and tears filled the air as he bestowed his benedictions before gently transferring the body into a waiting vehicle destined for the graveyard. We embarked on a solemn journey towards our final destination, tears streaming down our faces as grief consumes us all. The burial site came into view and we carefully carried my father's remains to their resting place. Accompanied by some of his closest friends, we stood by as prayers were recited and then laid him to rest. It was in that fleeting moment, that last glimpse of his handsome face and form, that I reflected upon both the pain he had caused us and found forgiveness within my heart. A pang of longing surged through me; if only I could turn back time and grant him another chance at life! Instead, I beseech God with fervent prayers for forgiveness on behalf of my father's transgressions against me and our family. I pleaded for his eternal happiness. As I peered into the grave where his mortal remains would forever rest, I whispered silent words from deep within my heart...

Dad, you're my ultimate hero. You've raised me with such wisdom and care. Why can't you see that? Yes, I may make mistakes, but it doesn't mean I'm a terrible person. I have strong values and a clear sense of right and wrong. I know who I am and I'm growing into the person I want to be. Look, you didn't do everything perfectly, but as you've always taught me, doing your best is what truly matters. The most valuable life lessons I've learned have come from you. Does it matter if I can spell or solve an equation? You'd tell me it's not important at all. What truly matters is what's in my heart, who I am as a person and the positive impact I make on the world around me. None of us are perfect, not even you, and you never pretended to be flawless. And for that honesty and authenticity, Dad, I love you even more. So please take your wise advice and go easy on yourself because no one expects you to be the perfect parent. But let me assure you that you were far from being the worst either; not by a long shot! Why can't you comprehend this? Yes, there were mistakes along the way but what truly counts is that despite them all, you never gave up on being there for me. And for that unwavering commitment alone, Dad...I love you endlessly!

After the burial of my father's body, everyone offered their blessings, embraced us, and departed. We too made our way back home, but I couldn't bring myself to enter. Instead,

I longed to sit by his grave once again and share laughter through our favourite comedies. How I yearned to have him back in my life! It was incredibly painful to accept that he had taken his own life. Didn't he realize that his daughter still cherished him? Why did he make this irreversible decision? The weight of these questions brought tears streaming down my face.

Frustration consumed me as I questioned the unfairness of life itself. Nothing seemed capable of soothing the anguish within me; being different from others only intensified my sense of isolation. Each moment of that day felt unbearable, and if only I possessed some supernatural power, I would have resurrected my dad without hesitation. However, in my heartache, I also blamed myself for not expressing how much he meant to me before it was too late. Anger towards myself mingled with grief as I pondered how Dad could leave me so alone in this desolate world.

He was the sole individual who could effortlessly bring a smile to my face when sadness enveloped me. He was the person with whom I enjoyed conversing wholeheartedly. His unwavering support ensured that all my desires were fulfilled without hesitation or complaint. Even though singing wasn't a strong suit of mine, he encouraged me relentlessly to pursue it nonetheless. Our playful game sessions were filled with his infectious humour and an unwavering desire for me to emerge victorious each time we played together. His jokes never failed to elicit laughter from deep within me. Whenever failure struck, he consoled me by urging another attempt next time around. His capacity for forgiveness knew no bounds; he never held grudges against me for even a moment's lapse in judgment or action on my part. He possessed an unwavering faith in my abilities, something that no one else seemed to possess. I miss the warm embraces, the tender kisses, and the abundant love that only he could provide. His culinary skills were unparalleled, and his compliments about my unique beauty resonated deeply within me. He embraced me just as I was, accepting me without reservation or condition. And now, I find myself bereft of anyone who can offer such heartfelt praise.

I returned to my abode and penned this heartfelt poem in his honour.

As I traverse the streets, reminiscences of our time together persistently linger,
Each step I take brings me closer to witnessing a father with his daughter,
A sight that evokes memories of my remarkable father.

Whenever I cast my mind back, the recollections of you continue to haunt me,
Your fondness for comedy films, those days filled with endless laughter.

Alcohol and cigarettes were your constant companions,
But it was your smile that held immeasurable worth for me.
Your words, cherished then and now, are forever etched in my heart.

Sometimes, gazing at the vast expanse of sky above,
I ponder why you departed so swiftly without seeking my consent.
Why did fate decree that I become a fatherless child,
Left alone in this desolate world devoid of parental guidance?

Since your departure, tears have ceaselessly cascaded from my eyes,
The love you bestowed upon me remains indelible.
Finding someone capable of loving me as deeply as you did has proven arduous.
Oh how deeply I adore you, Daddy.

I never got to say goodbye to my father. The words were there, lingering on the tip of my tongue, but I couldn't bring myself to speak them. The tears in his eyes, the frailty in his voice, they told me everything I needed to know. He was leaving me, slipping away into the unknown, and there was nothing I could do to stop it.

I watched him fade before my eyes, his once strong frame now a mere shadow of its former self. The memories flooded back, of a time when he was my hero, my protector, my everything. How could I say goodbye to the man who had shaped me, who had taught me right from wrong, who had loved me unconditionally?

As I held his hand for the last time, I felt a wave of emotions wash over me. Regret, for all the things left unsaid. Gratitude, for all the moments we had shared. And love, a love so deep and profound that it transcended words.

And as he took his final breath, I whispered a silent goodbye, knowing that he would always be with me, in my heart, in my memories, in every beat of my soul. Goodbye, my unforgettable father. You will never be forgotten.

XI

After Dad

Life had undergone a remarkable transformation. We were finally liberated from the anguish and constraints that held us back. There was no longer anything to worry about. Our existence had been restored, and with it came a renewed sense of passion for one another. My love for him had never waned; it had merely become overshadowed by the pain of losing my father. Wherever my father may be now, I believe he would find solace in witnessing his beloved wife and the man she loves living together, leading a contented life filled with love, banter, and happiness. Without any regrets, I divulged my past - although it seemed unfamiliar to others, it was all too familiar to me. Time had brought about healing for some wounds while leaving others untouched.

Life was now different without my father's presence. Every little aspect of our lives had changed. There was a tinge of loneliness within me. The harsh reality that I would never lay eyes on my father again settled in. All the arguments and anxieties were now things of the past as we embarked on a fresh start in life. It wasn't that we found joy in our father's departure; rather, something within us shifted entirely after his passing. I could sense that change deep within me. Even today, I feel as though my father is still alive - accompanying me wherever I go and whatever I do. He exists somewhere out there, patiently waiting for our reunion, perhaps in heaven. His memories haunted me wherever I ventured. His essence seemed to manifest itself in various individuals around me; whenever loneliness or sadness engulfed me, his presence lingered like an invisible embrace. The fragrance he used to wear still permeated the air anywhere I went.

Finally bidding farewell to the house we temporarily resided in, we returned to our own home - the place where Dad once lived with us. We rearranged our belongings throughout the day until everything found its rightful place. Occasionally, I yearned for my father to reenter my life and fill the void that remained within me. However, I knew deep down that this wish was futile. Life without my father was monotonous and overwhelmingly lonely. I despised going to school; there were no true friends to rely on, only a handful of acquaintances. It seemed as though everyone held some level of disdain towards me, maybe because of my short temper and tendency to take things seriously.

People took me for granted and never showed any concern for my well-being. But I didn't care one bit; all I did was focus on studying. Life throws curveballs, but we must carry on! If only others could comprehend the kind of friends I had in life... It saddens me when people fail to perceive the emotions that others experience. Instead of offering support, they feign care while pushing you down into the ground - observing your downfall with laughter... People seldom grasp the true essence of friendship. Throughout my life, I will continue believing that "friends" are often individuals who masquerade as allies but harbour hidden identities as foes. When will my friends truly become genuine companions? It remains a mystery.

I wish... oh how I wish... that I could rewind time and return to an era when everything was flawless. A time when judgment from others didn't exist when our only source of pain was scraped knees from falling over when we were still our fathers' darlings when everyone around us felt like a friend - a time when we had the freedom to be whomever we desired without being labelled or judged. Why did it all change? Why did we have to grow up? And more importantly, why did our innocence have to be snatched away so mercilessly - at such a tender age? Why does no one see beyond the facade of fake smiles and laughter concealing the pain and tears that accompany me every single day? Not even our own family or most of our friends can fathom it.

Why do we keep so much of our lives hidden from our loved ones? Why can't they see that all the yelling, arguing, and fighting are hurting us? For me, education always took precedence. The future could wait. Sometimes, I struggled to focus on my studies at school because my father's thoughts would constantly distract me in different directions. Out of all my teachers, the only one I truly admired was my English teacher. She had a calm and caring demeanour that made her stand out. While some teachers were strict when it came to academics, they could also be sweet.

Life continued moving forward, but I despised everything around me. I hated my school, my friends, my teachers - even my father for leaving me. I detested the loneliness and negativity that surrounded me. At school, I never paid much attention to studying because I knew deep down that I would still pass with good grades. My friends were always drawn to the attractive guys in our school.

After completing 10th grade, I missed everything - my school, friends, and teachers. I longed for the fun times we used to have when teachers weren't around - laughing together and joking about cute guys passing by us. I missed copying answers during unit tests without getting caught by our oblivious teacher. Even the moments spent gossiping in the restroom while waiting for class to end held a certain nostalgia for me.

I yearn to go back to those shared moments - the parties with friends and blaring music; the mischievous times spent in the principal's office; when he held me close and professed his love for God as his witness; returning to the house where childhood memories were made; revisiting those spots where we played imaginary games. All these memories remain treasured in a past that seems unreachable now; it's difficult to move on while still holding onto them tightly. But someday, maybe that phone will ring and they'll call, saying, "Come back home, we've all been missing you. You are the company we seem to lack."

I seemed to miss everything, and during my vacations, I always felt lonely at home with nothing to do. I would glance down at my arms and see the scars - a reminder of the nights I cried, wishing it was all just a dream. Little did I know that things were even worse than they appeared. None of my friends bothered to check if I was okay or alive. It was in those moments that I realized I was being taken for granted and not appreciated for who I truly am or the kindness in my heart. Did they even know that I had a heart?

Entering high school brings about significant changes in one's life. It's a time when even the closest friends can transform, turning into someone completely different. The once mundane act of doing homework is now disregarded, and cell phones become a common sight in classrooms. Detention escalates to suspension, and innocent soda is replaced by beer. Even something as simple as chewing gum takes on a new form as it becomes associated with pot. Bicycles are traded for cars, and lollipops are swapped for cigarettes. Lip gloss is replaced by makeup, marking a shift in priorities and appearances. Yes, high school has an undeniable impact on everyone. During this time, my friends seemed to forget that I even existed in their lives. Meanwhile, my thoughts became more twisted and chaotic. I would try to suppress my screams of sorrow while dreading the arrival of each new day.

Gradually, I lost my appetite and found solace only in self-inflicted pain. Back then, my trusty blade was there for me when no one else was around. However, I couldn't escape the dark cloud that loomed over me. Those were the days when nobody understood, Nobody comprehended the pain that consumed me, Nobody grasped the challenges life had thrown at me, Nobody saw the tears that constantly streamed from my eyes, And all they ever fed me were lies. Eventually, they stopped acknowledging my existence altogether.

Before delving further into this topic, it's crucial to acknowledge how influential our closest relationships are in shaping who we become. Take a moment to think about three individuals who have had a profound impact on you - these are often the people whose traits manifest within our behaviour subtly but significantly. The value of authentic friendships cannot be overstated; true friends don't begrudge your success but instead celebrate it wholeheartedly while having unwavering faith in your abilities - quality always outweighs quantity in this regard. When choosing those closest to you, pay attention to their manner of speaking. It is through their words that one can discern both maturity and character.

After my father left, I underwent a profound transformation, becoming someone entirely new - a fresh start, if you will. I am far from perfect, fully aware of my flaws. More often than not, my smiles are mere facades designed to conceal the pain I endure silently. Only my mother and brother bear witness to my tears; they are the ones with whom I share my deepest thoughts because they understand me better than anyone else ever could. It frustrates me when people assume they know everything about me when in reality, I struggle to comprehend myself fully. My identity seems to change daily; mood swings are an inherent part of who I am.

I will dedicate my utmost efforts to bring happiness to my

friends and family. As a teenager, I am bound to make numerous mistakes in life, just as I have already done. The changes I undergo are for myself, sometimes leading to improvement, other times not so much, but ultimately it is for my growth. Naturally, everyone expects me to be a well-behaved young lady. However, the truth is that I am both good and bad. Frankly speaking, I couldn't care less about what people say or think about me because they should ensure their perfection before passing judgment on me. Interestingly enough, I find it amusing when others imitate me as it brings attention to my unique ideas. No one can ever truly describe who I am; trust me when I say that there is nothing peculiar about me. I am UNIQUE! It's not about being pretty or intelligent or perfect - none of those apply to me. Instead, what matters most is embracing my authentic self and loving every aspect of who I am! If you don't appreciate that, well then go straight to hell!

Just like everyone else, I have feelings too. Despite being flawed at times, remember that beneath it all, I am still human. All I desire is love - love for who I truly am and love for the talents that define me. It is during moments of solitude that I find solace and rejuvenate myself. My life may seem like one big joke or a whimsical dance with spoken melodies; the laughter fills me so intensely that it almost becomes overwhelming when reflecting upon myself. While acknowledging myself as a creation of God, it is equally important for me to recognize and acknowledge others as creations of God as well. Oh! There's one more thing worth mentioning: My purpose in life revolves around loving and supporting My Mom, My Dad (may he rest in peace), and My Brother!

These individuals hold immense significance in my life, and I make it a point to shower them with love every single moment! Losing them is something I cannot bear, just like the loss of my dear father. However, I must admit that when they are not around for even a day, it feels as though a part of me is missing. The absence of my father weighs heavily on my heart. He was more than just a parent; he was someone I could not imagine living without. Among all the people in my life, there is no one else I miss more than him. The memories of his smile, warm hugs, and shared laughter while watching Munnabhai still linger within me. And most importantly, I simply MISS HIM.

Ever since my dad passed away, there has been an undeniable void in my heart. It dawned on me just how special he was to me - someone irreplaceable and essential to my existence. No one else's absence has affected me as profoundly as he did. The last words he uttered to me were "I'm sorry." Oh, how I longed to make him feel cherished and valued! If only I could have embraced him tightly and conveyed that he was an extraordinary person worthy of admiration. My intention was for him to understand that his daughter still loved him unconditionally and would always be there for him. There were so many things left unlearned between us before his untimely departure from this world. How could he abandon his daughter like this? Did he ever consider the unbearable loneliness that would consume me? If only there had been something capable of changing his decision; then perhaps he would still be alive today. I will forever love and cherish the memories of my dad - My Daddy taught me three fundamental principles: First, fight for what you believe in even if you find yourself standing alone; secondly, fight for what you deserve; and last but most importantly, fight for what you love. As long as I adhere to these three principles, everything will be alright.

Feeling humiliated and the fear of humiliation, breaking out in sweats and then being even more embarrassed by the sweats while feeling like everyone is staring at them - it's a snowball effect. Being alone brings relaxation and a sense of being unwatched and unjudged. It's a deeply sad thing to live with, especially in my case. Our minds are constantly racing, judging ourselves, trying to change and relax ourselves, understand who we are, label ourselves, and find our place in this world. This is just a glimpse of the roller coaster that runs through our brains without rest. It's truly a terrible disorder. We are cool people; we just can't help it. A "normal" person may experience incredible sadness when losing a loved one or intense fear during a traffic collision or when given a large respB sensibility. Now imagine all these feelings combined into one person every second of every day for their entire life. It's intense! I opened my diary and poured out my feelings.

Dear daddy,

Do you realize what could have been prevented if you had stayed with us? No, of course, you don't realize it because you're gone - just a ghost from my memories.

People sometimes ask me if I remember you being around, and I always say no because while I do remember the good times we shared, what stands out most are those last few months. You know, the months when you threw Mom across the room and choked Reynolds.

We went to the park every weekend - you, me, brother - playing badminton together. I used to have fun, Daddy. Do you want to know what my life is like now? I hang out with my so-called friends and cry to them. I could stay and finish school, get hit on by idiotic guys in stupid bars that let me in, get a job as a waitress somewhere, and wait for the day when some jerk is just nice enough to win my heart. I could do all of that. Or I could go somewhere new, be someone new, and meet people who won't judge me based on my past. I could meet a nice boy who will love me no matter what I've been through and one day blame you for the terrible childhood and worst nightmares you gave me. Daddy, what do I do? You're not here to hold me while I cry. The tears falling down my face as I think of you hurt. You left me all alone with only memories - pictures of you and me growing up under your loving care. You left me here to fend for myself with only the words "I love you." I miss you with all my heart, and sometimes it feels like no one else cares. Watching Mom move on like you were never here hurts. It's as if she never loved us or relied on us when we needed her support. Daddy, I don't know what to do; living without you is unbearable. No matter how many times I try to get through a day without feeling this pain, deep down inside, I know it's impossible. Now more than ever before, it's clear that living without you was never meant for me - loneliness will always be by my side.

Mom is already involved with someone else, and I know you're aware of that, right? It's because you didn't fulfil her desires. However, he provides her with everything she wants. Why, Dad? Why? He is reminiscent of you in various ways, someone she spends all her time with as if he were everything. She laughs and jokes around as if this man were you, and silently I wish it were! What should I do, Daddy? I want Mom to be happy, but not at the expense of introducing someone new into our lives. I miss you so much that it pains me to see her like this while knowing you're watching over us. I long for the day when we can be reunited and embrace each other like we used to. The tears stream down my cheeks as memories of you flood my mind, making it difficult to breathe. I know I should be content, but the tears continue to fall and the pain remains unbearable. Daddy, please help me. What am I supposed to do?

You are my hero, my protector, my teacher – my father whom I hold dear in my heart. Although your absence on Earth is deeply felt, deep down inside me resides the knowledge that one day we will embark on a new journey together. You guided me through life from the moment of my birth until you departed from this world. This message serves as a heartfelt communication from me to you. So here we are now – if indeed you are reading this letter – Daddy; it seems that curiosity got the better of you and led you back into our lives momentarily just to witness how things have turned out for me. Well then...now perhaps you can see that happiness can exist without your presence by observing how well-adjusted and content I have become in your absence. Although it took some time for me to come to this realization, rest assured that I will be alright without you – yes, I will be alright.

Nevertheless, my love for you remains unwavering.

With love,
Rene.

I closed my diary and gently wiped away the few tears that had escaped. It only takes a minute to develop a crush on someone, an hour to develop affection towards them, and a day to fall in love with them. But it takes a lifetime to forget someone. It is natural to feel sadness when we lose someone dear to us – whether it's a close relative or even a beloved pet. That kind of sadness has its unique name – grief. No matter what challenges we face or how much we may argue, I will always love my mom and my brother because I know that they will always be there for me in the end. Moving on may seem simple, but it's leaving behind what truly makes it difficult. Trying to forget someone you once loved is like attempting to remember someone you never had the chance to know. Instead of dwelling on what's over, let's find solace in the fact that we were fortunate enough to have experienced it at all. Sometimes, when you miss someone dearly, the entire world seems empty and devoid of life. That saying holds – "You never know what you have until it's gone."

A letter from my friend calms me.

Hey Rene,

I just wanted to take a moment to express my heartfelt gratitude for all the ways you've supported me. I must admit, I've never received such incredible assistance before in my entire life. Your unwavering support means the world to me, and I truly hope that you never change, no matter what. You know, it's quite puzzling to me. Despite my father's kindness and all the good he has done for others, his business seems to be struggling. It used to be that whatever he wished for would come true, but now it feels like everything is going in the opposite direction. It's hard for me to comprehend why good people often end up suffering in the end. Karma can be quite unforgiving at times. With that being said, I humbly ask for a favour from you. Would you please pray for our business? I truly believe that with your prayers and positive energy, our business will thrive and make significant progress in the future. On a personal note, I have a wish for you as well - if you'll permit me.

My greatest desire is to see a perpetual smile on your face. Remember, nothing can hurt you unless you allow it to power over your emotions. May your path always lead you towards success and may you shine like a golden star in your own life. Being around you brings about an incredible sense of warmth and joy, and I feel incredibly fortunate to have the opportunity to learn from someone as amazing as you. Thank you for always being there when I needed someone to talk to or lean on during difficult times. You are truly the best friend I've ever had in my life; words cannot adequately describe how grateful I am for your presence. Please know that everything shared within this letter is meant only between us; confidentiality is of utmost importance here. Wishing you all the best in your future endeavours.

Sending love and light,
Mia

XII

Dazzling Diamond Ring. Mr Right

Once upon a time, there was a magnificent diamond ring that captivated everyone's attention. It was truly an extraordinary piece of jewellery, radiating brilliance and elegance. This remarkable ring had the power to make hearts skip a beat and ignite feelings of love and desire.

The story revolves around a gentleman named Mr. Right, who is on a quest to find the perfect ring for his beloved. He wanted something that would symbolize their eternal bond and express his deep affection for her. As he embarked on his search, Mr. Right found himself in a world full of sparkling gems and dazzling displays. Each jewellery store he visited showcased an array of exquisite rings, but none seemed to embody the essence of his love. However, fate had something special in store for him.

One fateful day, while strolling through the streets adorned with twinkling lights, he stumbled upon a small boutique tucked away in an alley. Intrigued by its quaint charm, he decided to step inside. To his amazement, the boutique housed an extraordinary collection of unique and enchanting rings. The owner greeted him warmly and guided him towards a display case that held the most captivating diamond ring he had ever laid eyes on.

As Mr. Right held the ring in his hands, he could feel its energy resonating with his soul. It was as if this ring was meant to be theirs—an emblem of their profound connection. With excitement coursing through his veins, Mr. Right knew that this dazzling diamond ring would be the one to sweep his beloved off her feet. Its exquisite craftsmanship and radiant sparkle were unmatched by any other piece he had encountered on his journey.

Filled with anticipation and joyous butterflies fluttering within him, Mr Right prepared himself to propose to his beloved with this stunning symbol of their love story—a testament to their everlasting commitment. In conclusion, this tale highlights the extraordinary power that lies within a single piece of jewellery—a testament to the magic of love and the lengths one will go to find the perfect symbol for their beloved.

I've always had this vivid imagination of what it would be like when the love of my life pops the question, you know? I'm talking about a scene straight out of a romantic movie - a gorgeous diamond ring, my Mr. Right down on one knee, and a breathtaking backdrop. Just thinking about it gives me goosebumps! I mean, don't we all daydream about such things? It's totally normal, right? I've heard parents say that it's just part of growing up after hitting puberty. They claim that during this phase, we experience so many emotions and thoughts because we're maturing. Honestly, sometimes I wish we could just skip past all this puberty stuff. Life was so much simpler when we were kids. We didn't have to worry about much; others took care of everything for us. But wasn't it the opposite back then? We were so eager to grow up and do all those adult things! And now that we're here, it's not exactly what we expected! Can life get any more complicated? Is it too much to ask for a perfect and uncomplicated life? Well, here's one thing I've learned - life goes on.

From spending nine months in our mother's womb to finally entering this world; childbirth is no easy feat for mothers. For those initial nine months, there wasn't much to worry about because our every need was taken care of and our lives were protected even before we arrived in this world. But when the time came for us to enter the world... oh boy, let me tell you, mothers go through immense pain. Two years ago, I thought I knew what love truly meant. Now as I sit here writing these words, I'm starting to realize that love means being willing to do anything for someone - even sacrificing your own life if necessary. It means feeling an unbreakable bond with that person and being completely comfortable around them. No matter how many fights you have or what you argue about, they will never leave your side, and you won't leave theirs. That, my friend, is love. That's what life is all about.

Love... isn't it a beautiful word? It's about being surrounded by people who know exactly how to make you happy and are willing to do anything for your happiness. They're always there for you, even when you don't ask for it. It's the realization of just how much that person means to you!

That's real love. I learned all this from the incredible individuals in my life who showed me what true love really is. Now, who are these people? Well, I guess you'll find out... later! All I can say is that I feel incredibly blessed throughout my almost 18 years on this earth because of them. They've shaped me into the person I am today and will continue to influence me tomorrow and forever.

ꙮ

"Rene, honey! Come downstairs before you're late for college!" My mom's voice echoed from the cosy kitchen downstairs, interrupting my train of thought. Looks like my daydreaming took over again! Maybe today will be different; who knows? With a yawn escaping my lips, I made my way downstairs to join my mom.

"Good morning," she greeted me with a warm smile as I leaned in to kiss her cheek.

"Good morning, Mom," I greeted as I grabbed a slice of toast. "You do realize you're running late, right?" Mom's voice grew stern.

"Sorry, mom. I was... hawww!" I stifled a yawn mid-sentence.

"I'm off to work. Have a great day." She kissed me and headed towards the door.

"Finish your breakfast and don't forget to leave."

"I love you, mom." "Where's Rey?" I inquired.

"Oh, he already left for college," she replied before

disappearing from sight.

I wasn't particularly hungry, so I quickly ate some toast and gulped down a glass of orange juice before heading out. Normally, mom wouldn't let me leave without breakfast since she believed it was an essential meal to fuel my energy for the day. But today was an exception. Fifteen minutes later, I arrived at college. As I walked towards the college building, my gaze wandered across the campus yard where students were engaged in various activities. It had become somewhat of a habit for me to observe people; it fascinated me. Everything seemed ordinary at first glance - students chatting, laughing, eating... hold on! Something seemed off. Some were even studying outside their designated classrooms. Were they lost? Did I accidentally end up at the wrong college?

Just then, an announcement echoed through the campus speakers: "Dear students, love is our true destiny. We don't discover life's meaning alone; we find it with someone else. When you love someone deeply, all your hidden desires start surfacing. Love has the power to navigate through treacherous paths where fear lingers like wolves in the night. Where there is love, wishes always bloom. Today is Valentine's Day - a whole day dedicated solely to love itself! Does it make sense? Well... not really! Love can make us all go crazy but hey, it's also incredibly fun, isn't it? From the bottom of my heart, I wish you all a very happy Valentine's Day. Remember, if you learn to love yourself first, finding your Valentine becomes much easier! Let love spread today and every other day. Cheers..." I stood there, absorbing every word of the announcement. Damn it, I should have checked my calendar. I chuckled softly at my lack of awareness about Valentine's Day.

"You'll find your valentine soon," a familiar voice whispered softly in my ear.I let out a long, exaggerated squeal of excitement and wrapped my arms tightly around her.

"Happy Valentine's Day!" I exclaimed. She chuckled and returned the hug. "Same to you," she replied.

Then, with a mischievous grin, she asked, "Did you hear what I said earlier?"

Trying to change the subject, I asked casually, "Hey, do we have any classes today?"

She refused to let me evade the question. Her expression turned serious as she said firmly, "Don't change the topic, baby. Answer me."

My heart sank as I realized I might be in trouble. Nervously swallowing a lump in my throat, I took a step back.

Not giving it much thought, I blurted out with a blush on my cheeks, "Yeah... yeah, I heard you."

Curious and playful, she winked and asked teasingly, "Well then? What about it?"

Feeling slightly overwhelmed by the situation and desperately trying to lighten the mood, I waved my hands in the air and said defensively, "Oh come on! I'm just 16! Still a kid! And besides... we go to an 'ALL GIRLS COLLEGE' if you haven't noticed."

Mia didn't react immediately. Instead, she took my hand and led me to our secret spot—the terrace of our college building. We always retreated there whenever we needed privacy for our conversations. "You need someone special in your life," Mia began earnestly. She looked deep into my eyes as if searching for something within me. "Someone who can love you unconditionally... someone who can bring happiness into your life... You deserve love in its purest form." She paused for effect before pointing at one of our teachers nearby and continued passionately,"Look at Miss Montgomery over there... Do you really want to end up like her? Unmarried and constantly depressed? Can't you see the toll it has taken on her She's become a spinster because she never found true love... And I don't want that for you. Life is about beautiful experiences, the feeling of loving someone and being loved in return."

We both knew that it was now my turn to respond. The weight of her words hung in the air, waiting for my answer. I took a deep breath, trying to find the right words to express myself. I wasn't fully prepared for this conversation, but deep down, I knew that not everyone is destined for a successful love story.

"Mia," I finally spoke up, "I've witnessed what love does to people... and what happens after they get married... It scares me... MARRIAGE scares me! Trust me, I've seen the worst of it. My parents' constant fights and objects flying around our house... My dad's alcohol-fueled outbursts and my mom's disregard for our well-being... My dad didn't care about anything that was happening...Their conflicts escalated to such an extreme level that it became completely unbearable for them to coexist any longer. They had reached the point where they were almost willing to harm themselves. At some stage, I came to understand that parents have the option to separate, divorce, or live apart from each other. I sensed that we were approaching that moment. It felt like everything was coming to an end. All I wanted was a stable and loving family, but damn it, I was too young to comprehend the reasons behind their arguments. Every night, I experienced intense emotional pain that tormented my mind. For the past 13 years of my life, until his passing, I learned how to cope with this torture. I've witnessed pain and suffering firsthand and it's something I desperately want to avoid. It's not just about me; I've seen countless relationships crumble due to breakups and infidelity. Mia, you don't understand how difficult it is...I'm scared...I don't want any more pain...I yearn for happiness but at the same time, fear falling in love again...I've lost so much already - people who were important in my life - and I can't bear the thought of losing anyone else like how I lost my father...You don't know much about it...you've always been so happy...you have a perfect family, a perfect house, a perfect boyfriend - your life is filled with pleasure and indulgence...What more could you possibly want?" My words flowed nonstop as I struggled to catch my breath between sentences; it felt suffocating trying to convey all this emotion.

Despite attempting a calm tone of voice, everyone's eyes were fixed on us - especially me as if they believed I was at fault here. Without exchanging another word or making eye contact with anyone, I stormed off the terrace, grabbed my bag hastily and walked away while tears still lingered on my cheeks. I heard Mia calling out to me, but I wasn't ready to face her again. I craved solitude. I longed for the comfort of my home. I needed my mom; I wanted to embrace her and feel reassured that everything would eventually be alright. Now, everyone knows...I let out a sigh, covering my face with embarrassment as I sat cross-legged on my bed in my room. It's not the time to cry now; it would only make me appear weak. Well, that's my weakness - recalling the painful memories of my past and all the excruciating moments, especially the loss of my dad and leaving behind my best friend...just thinking about it hurts! Oh well, I haven't really delved into the reasons behind why we drifted apart.

Ah, let's delve into yet another painful memory, shall we? It's rather amusing how life has a way of playing ironic tricks on us. I'm currently in the process of erasing every trace of him from my mind, although there was a time when he held the position of my closest and most trusted companion. However, as if following the tired clichés of a cheesy film, fate took an unexpected turn. Moving on proved to be an incredibly challenging undertaking, one that demanded an immense amount of strength and unwavering determination. Alas, it was a necessary step that simply couldn't be avoided...

XIII

Throwback to 6th Grade

As I transitioned into sixth grade, I discovered that I had been placed in a specialized education category within my school. This particular category was designated for students who encountered obstacles in their studies or possessed some form of cognitive impairment that hindered their academic engagement. The situation was quite perplexing for me since I perceived myself as an ordinary twelve-year-old experiencing the typical changes of adolescence. It was difficult to comprehend why I was being labeled as someone with a mental disability when there was no evidence to support such a claim. Naturally, no one is flawless and we all possess our own imperfections, but this classification felt unjust and unfair.

It seemed unfair that children like me were segregated from the mainstream education system just because we didn't fit into their definition of "normal." Why couldn't they see that it was a form of torture? Why couldn't they place us alongside students with a similar IQ level? I questioned my own identity and searched through my medical records, birth certificate, and baptism records, hoping to find an explanation for this situation. But no answer could be found. The concept of "special education" scared me immensely, although I couldn't quite pinpoint why. It felt as if my brain was constantly being pierced by a dagger, causing immense frustration and pain within me. I tried to keep these feelings hidden inside, but they slowly ate away at me every second of every minute. It felt like my heart and soul were bleeding profusely from the wounds inflicted upon them by this unjust segregation. The pain consumed me completely.

I often wondered why things had to be this way. Why did society subject me to years of suffering without any justification? Wasn't there anyone who could hear my cries for help? Sadly, it seemed impossible to rise above these circumstances and bring about change in my lifetime. To make matters worse, even my once-upon-a-time friends turned against me after being placed in the special education category. They distanced themselves from me, treating me as if I were invisible. Their judgmental behavior hurt deeply because it made me feel like I was no longer normal in their eyes. It was disheartening to realize that they had changed their views about me solely based on this categorization. I began to doubt myself and lost faith in my abilities. Negative thoughts overwhelmed me, causing feelings of nausea and claustrophobia. However, amidst all the turmoil, I came across the concept of karma and the saying "What goes around, comes around." I decided to leave it up to karma and focus on being a good human being. I resolved to study to the best of my ability and prove my worth by excelling in my academics. No challenges would deter me; it was simply a matter of embracing my true nature. After being assigned to my class, I learned that unlike students in the mainstream education system who had seven subjects, I would only be studying six subjects - English, Hindi, Math, Science, Social Studies, and Computers.

In the world of mainstream education, there were typically seven subjects to study. However, I had the fortunate circumstance of not having to study Kannada, which was an additional subject. The idea of not having to study it brought a sense of relief and joy. Honestly, I didn't particularly enjoy that subject; it was quite boring. Now looking back, I regret not taking the opportunity to study it because as a resident of Karnataka, it was important for me to be familiar with the state's language. I feel a bit ashamed now because while I can understand Kannada, I'm not very fluent in speaking it. Although I was excited about my other subjects, I wasn't entirely happy with my surroundings at that time.

We were introduced to a new class called "Life Skills," where we would learn about manners, values, positive thinking, and awareness. It sounded quite interesting. Additionally, we were told that we would have sports and fine arts classes where we would interact with students from the mainstream education system. Of course, we would cooperate with them; however, it felt a bit awkward being around them knowing that we were labeled as "special students" due to our learning disabilities. Speaking of learning disabilities... What a joke! Before being categorized as "special children," I was initially placed in the "Learning Enhancement" category along with some popular students who struggled academically but still had above-average intelligence levels (though not at an excellent level). Students who performed below average were considered "special students." The principal reconsidered and decided that being in the "Special Learning" category would be more beneficial for me as my studies would receive more attention and importance while having fewer classmates—around 5 to 20 students per class. This news didn't sit well with me; it felt like pure bad luck. I wanted my friends by my side—it didn't seem fair at all!

It made me want to cry and fight against this unjust situation.

The first day of 6th grade is still etched in my memory. I entered the classroom with nervousness, my palms sweaty. I took a seat and placed my bag to the right, rubbing my palms anxiously, hoping to calm my nerves. I was the first one to arrive; there was no one else around. As I observed the classroom, I noticed six benches in shades of light brown and white, a window to my right, a large blackboard in front of me with chalk and an eraser hanging from its side pockets. The walls were painted white with a brownish-black glass door covering them. It suddenly dawned on me that if there were only six benches, it meant that there would only be six students in my class! Wow! This was something different—a smaller class size meant more fun. But then I quickly snapped myself out of those thoughts; this wasn't about having fun or leisure time. This was about being serious and focusing on studying.

"You need to concentrate," I scolded myself silently as I let out a sigh.

I was about to meet five more extraordinary students. Glancing at my watch, I noticed it was already 8:00 AM. Letting out a sigh, I rested both hands on the desk and placed my head on top, closing my eyes. It wasn't that I wanted to sleep; I just needed a moment to relax. After less than five minutes, I heard footsteps approaching, causing me to jump in surprise. A shadow appeared before me, and from its silhouette, I could tell it was a girl. The shadow revealed two braided plaits of hair, a bag slung over her right shoulder, an oval-shaped face, slender arms and legs, and a lean figure resembling that of a skeleton. Well, that's what it seemed like. The shadow followed the path towards my classroom as I shivered slightly and turned my gaze towards the blackboard in an attempt to ignore her presence. The sound of footsteps grew louder until finally coming to a stop near me. Slowly turning my head towards her direction, our eyes met as she smiled at me warmly. Returning the smile with equal warmth.

"Are you Rene?" she asked softly. I widened my eyes and furrowed my eyebrows in surprise - how did she know my name?

"Yes, that's me," I responded somewhat foolishly. Instead of asking for her name in return - how silly of me.

"Well actually," she replied with a smile while extending her hand towards mine "Each classroom door displays photos along with the names of all the students in our class."

"I'm Elena," she introduced herself as we shook hands.

"You have such a lovely name," I couldn't help but let out an appreciative sigh. "Thank you! Same goes for you," Elena said cheerfully

"You can call me Ellie if you'd like."

"I'm Rene... but you can call me anything you'd like..." I murmured quietly. "

Okay," she paused, lost in thought for a brief moment "I'll go with Rens; it sounds awesome."

I nodded, offering a small smile. Describing Elena, I could tell she was a total extrovert - the complete opposite of me, an introvert. She had a wheatish complexion and her hair was neatly oiled, almost covering her oval-shaped face. Her body appeared thin, like that of a skeleton. Her skirt reached up to her thighs while mine extended much longer past my knees. I covered the rest of my legs with school socks and shoes, as well as my hands and chest with a tracksuit to avoid any unwanted attention or stares. It felt like wearing a burqa, but strangely enough, it made me feel comfortable and light. At least I wouldn't have to endure those leering eyes that disgusted me so much. Trust me; I've witnessed far too many instances of that happening. Under such circumstances, I couldn't help but feel uncomfortable.

The Purdah system, which was once enforced by Muslims and some traditional Hindu families, seems like a thing of the past. It's rare to find anyone following it these days, especially Muslim women and certain Hindu families. I was reminded of Eli while listening to her talk about her family and why she disliked being classified as a "Special child." She had strong beliefs in atheism and seemed friendly enough to potentially become a good friend. As she noticed my quiet nature, she asked if I didn't talk much.

Just then, the voices of four boys entered the classroom. They paid no attention to us and engaged in their own conversation about Pokemon and Power Rangers. Typical boys, I thought sarcastically. Eli suggested going outside for a while, and I agreed with a soft smile. As we walked together, I accidentally bumped into the glass door without realizing it was there. The boys chuckled at my clumsiness but I refrained from reacting. Deep down, though, I wished I could give them a taste of their own medicine someday. Before crashing into the glass door, Eli had already reached the hallway outside our classroom. It didn't take me long to catch up with her as she noticed my red nose from the impact.

"Am I seeing things or is your nose actually red?" she asked curiously.

I admitted that I had accidentally run into the glass door on our way out and felt a bit embarrassed about it. Thankfully, she didn't laugh at my misfortune like those boys did.

"I'm sorry they laughed at you," she said sympathetically. "But one day we'll see them stumble and join in laughter ourselves."

Her words brought a smile to my face. It was strange yet comforting to meet someone who shared similar thoughts.

Wasn't it too early to find such a friend? Eli had this rebellious image that set her apart from other girls, but I knew better than to get involved in any trouble.

I made a conscious effort to distance myself from that situation. The reminder of what happened was etched in my long-term memory, but unfortunately, it didn't stick for very long. For the next 15 minutes, I sat in silence, observing the students around me. Among them, I spotted a few friends from the mainstream. At that moment, I wished to disappear. I didn't want to face them or hear their words. However, instead of acknowledging my presence with a friendly greeting or questioning why I had moved, they completely ignored me and walked proudly to their class. It felt as if there was an invisible glass door separating us. I remained unaffected by their actions; deep down, I expected this outcome.

This was just the beginning though; what could possibly be worse? At that moment, all I knew was that Eli was my only friend. As I glanced at her, she seemed distant and lost in her own thoughts. "Ellie..." I gently tapped her shoulder.

"Hmm... yeah," she sighed while furrowing her brows. Then she asked a question that I wasn't ready to answer, "Have you ever experienced being ignored before?"

I understood why she asked this question; perhaps she had gone through something similar to. It felt unfair - why couldn't we be treated the same way as before? Why couldn't things remain unchanged? Being ignored by someone whom you were once close with and shared so much of your life with is like repeatedly stabbing your heart until it bleeds without feeling any pain at all. Back then, I had my own group of friends; we were inseparable and shared everything – our secrets, lunches, happinesses, sorrows – practically everything under the sun! But when you find yourself one step lower on the social ladder, that's when you realize people's true colors and there's nothing you can do about it except replay memories of those good times while your heart shatters with each passing second.

Haven't we all experienced being ignored at least once in our lives? When you realize that someone is purposely ignoring you, it's best not to bother them again. Don't make any effort, not even the slightest. You're simply not worth it. They will eventually realize your true worth, maybe not right away, but in due time. They'll understand what they've lost and regret the misery and pain they caused... but by then, it will be too late.

"EARTH TO Rene... Why are you so lost?" Eli's voice snapped me back to reality. I flinched.

"Sorry, I was just-" *RING RING RING RING RING RING RING RING RING RING* Before I could finish my sentence, the school bell rang loudly in my ear, signaling that it was time to rush to our class. I was relieved that the bell interrupted my speech; I wasn't even sure what I wanted to say to her anyway. My thoughts were scattered and explaining what was going on in my mind seemed impossible. Did I have an answer for her question? Well, maybe talking wasn't something I felt like doing at that moment - perhaps silence suited me better or maybe I was simply too lazy to open my mouth. I looked over at Eli and we exchanged nods before entering our class. The boys seemed unusually quiet as they sat down at their respective desks; it appeared as if the sound of the bell made them uneasy and nervous – almost as if we had walked into a library – causing a pin-drop silence in the classroom.

I found myself sitting in my usual spot, with Eli by my side. A strange mix of nervousness and nausea began to overwhelm me. I couldn't help but wonder what was happening to me. This was a completely unfamiliar feeling, and it felt incredibly strange. My stomach churned with unease, as if it were part of this cycle of nerves that had taken hold of me. The silence in the room was becoming increasingly awkward. It seemed like nobody wanted to break it. All I could hear were the heavy breaths filling the atmosphere of the classroom. The nervousness and fear were palpable among everyone present.

Suddenly, a male voice whispered in my ear, calling me "red nose." A shiver ran down my spine as confusion took over, causing my eyebrow to twitch involuntarily.

Who on earth was this person referring to me as "red nose"? I turned towards the direction from which the voice came. It was a boy - the first boy in class who had ever spoken to me. He had a fair complexion, not quite as fair as snow white but more like an Anglo-Indian complexion. His lips were pink and quivering, something that many girls seemed to find attractive. His black eyes were so shiny that you could see your reflection in them with great clarity. There was an air of danger about him; he exuded a bad boy image that fascinated most girls - though not myself, mind you! He often displayed narcissistic tendencies when he indulged in his own self-admiration based on his physical attributes and arrogant pride stemming from them. He was exactly the kind of guy that most girls found appealing - surprisingly even those who usually followed mainstream trends. I couldn't help but wonder what these other girls saw in him that I couldn't find attractive at all. I never considered him a friend; I wouldn't even entertain the thought of having any sort of friendship with him.

"I have a freaking name, you know!" I whispered-yelled at him, giving him a stern look. He tried to soften his gaze and pouted his lips, as if that would somehow convince me. As if!

"Yeah, I know... it sounds pretty freaky!!!" he replied in the same tone as mine.

My eyes widened and I furrowed my brow. What on earth did he mean by that? I felt an intense desire to punch him in the face and watch him bleed. I clenched my fist tightly and bit down on my lower lip out of anger. My heart started racing, as if it were about to explode at any moment. This aggressive streak was definitely something I inherited from my father - a trait that seemed to be etched into me permanently, impossible to escape or deny.

"Listen..." I began with frustration evident in my voice. What was his name again? Oh crap...

"It's Shawn," he said, smirking as if he could read my thoughts - as if that would impress me!

“Listen up, Shawn. If you want a pencil, you better ask for it politely and with respect, using my name correctly," I said firmly.

"Well, I couldn’t care less..." he replied coldly, rolling his eyes.

"Then you won’t get one... Your loss! Not my problem," I muttered with fake sympathy.

Isn’t this just ridiculous? It’s the first day of school and this guy doesn’t even have a pencil. Even a first-grader would come prepared with one, especially on the first day. This guy is really getting on my nerves now. I took out my notebook and prepared to take notes.

He let out a sigh as if he had no other choice. "Ms. Red Nose, can I please borrow a pencil from you?" His voice was slightly louder this time, catching the attention of the three other boys and Eli. I wanted to slam my book right in his face! What’s so weird about my name? Take a deep breath, Rene. You can handle this now, I sighed. It’s not over yet!

"Red nose?! Is that really your name? Sounds pretty strange," another boy with light brown hair remarked, looking straight at me. I noticed a watch on his wrist – it was the Fastrack watch that I had always wanted! Seeing it on TV had sparked an admiration in me that knew no bounds. I just had to find a way to get one for myself somehow. But soon enough, my admiration turned into infatuation when Rolex watches caught my eye. That’s when things got even crazier for me – well, what can I say? I‘m quite the tomboy!

"Yeah dude, that's what she said! She even mentioned how freaky it sounded," Shawn replied to him with a wink directed at me. My glare intensified. Without uttering a word, I gave him an evil smirk – there was no point in arguing with fools, especially fools like him. I opened my pouch and handed him a pencil, hoping he would just shut his... face. I mean, his MOUTH! I wanted to throw the pencil right at his face and watch him bleed.

"Awww... did that hit a nerve?" he looked at me with puppy dog eyes and high-fived the other boy. My anger was building up inside me. I really wanted to see him turn to ashes.

"Rens," Ellie nudged me with her elbow, making me look at her. "Relax, he's just trying to test your limits."

My limits? Especially on the first day of 6th grade? Who does this guy think he is?

"My limits?! Yeah, I'll show him what I'm made of. Who does he think he is, the school chairman?" I whispered angrily while clenching my fist.

"Calm down," Ellie retorted and paused. "He's not even worth it." I raised an eyebrow in confusion.

"Worth what?"

"Your temper, of course! Save it for another time! It's our first day – try not to ruin it," she smiled.

"Okay," I sighed as I leaned back in my seat. I hope this day flies by so that I can go home and watch a movie with Dad.

XIV

Mathematics - The Ultimate Nemesis.

Ah, the subject that sends chills down my spine. There's a reason why I've been placed here, and now it's time to take it seriously and strive for greatness. I have no choice but to buckle down and study. I've made up my mind to keep distractions at bay. It's a subject that demands utmost attention and dedication. I must wholeheartedly commit myself to studying it, leaving no room for distractions.

Television - Checked.
Facebook - Checked.
WhatsApp - Checked.

No more indulging in leisure activities, it's time to focus solely on studying. I can't help but ponder how I will navigate through these demanding circumstances. Will I emerge victorious? Well, let's not dwell on such uncertainties, Rens! I swiftly push aside these thoughts to avoid any further disillusionment or frustration.

Our class teacher was introduced to us. Mrs. Aarzi appeared strict and stern at first glance, but deep down, there seemed to be a softer side to her. However, as they say, "Don't judge a book by its cover," I refrained from sitting on the cynic's throne and passing judgment. She is a teacher who deserves respect for her efforts in helping us excel. Teachers teach us things even our parents don't know. They provide insights into the world from their own experiences while denying that it was part of their journey. We should be eternally grateful for their knowledge and guidance; they shape who we become!

To my dismay, she announced that she would be teaching us mathematics. My ultimate nemesis! It's my Achilles' heel indeed! This subject has the power to make me cry... How will I survive this studying disaster? Those formulas, those equations... they already send shivers down my spine. The thought of facing this subject fills me with shame... If only I could hide behind a door and become invisible! But alas, that's not an option. It didn't take long for me to get acquainted with the other students in the class.

Besides Shawn and his high-five partner, there were two other boys whom I felt comfortable around. The high-fiving boy was Kris! I must say, Kris was far superior to Shawn in countless ways. Tyler and Veron were the names of those two boys who never said a word to me ever since I ran into a glass door. All I heard from them was laughter! It may sound strange, but their laughter was quite endearing... though not at that moment when I crashed into the door. In due time, I began to bond with everyone in the class except for Shane. He could be quite a jerk at times and always found ways to annoy me, though not physically. Indirectly, he would try to get under my skin. And his nickname for me "Red Nose" remained unchanged. It became his habit to call me that, but somehow, I grew accustomed to it and managed to keep my temper in check. I discovered that Kris and Shane were best friends long before Ellie, Tyler, Veron, and I joined the class. They had been in special education since 1st grade, so their bond was strong from the start. Initially, everyone here was a stranger to me, but that soon changed as I got to know them better. They turned out to be friendly... even Shane had his moments of friendliness before reverting to being a jerk pid! You're probably wondering what "jerkpid" means; well, it's a combination of "jerk" and "stupid." That's exactly what he is and always will be!

Tyler was a unique individual, quite reserved in his demeanour. Unlike the other three boys, he wasn't particularly talkative, and that's something I truly admire about him. In times of need, he was always there to offer a helping hand without hesitation. Math was his forte, and he excelled in it like no other subject. The class teacher would shower him with praise for his exceptional skills in calculations. While he may not have been what one would call a 3 a.m. friend, he assured me that he would always be there as a friend whenever I needed him. I was grateful to have met someone like Tyler.

Now let me introduce you to an important person who completely turned my world upside down - Veron. Interestingly enough, we became friends only after I got to know the other three boys. Veron was undoubtedly an extrovert just like Ellie; it seemed as though they shared similar characteristics. However, there was something about him that drew me in - something that changed my perception of him entirely. It was his eyes; they spoke volumes and had an irresistible allure that made it difficult to look away from your reflection within them. Many girls found him adorably cute, myself included (haha!). I found myself attracted to everything about Veron - his eyes, hair, cuteness, jokes, laughter...the list goes on and on. But it wasn't just physical attraction; there was also an emotional connection between us that I hadn't anticipated. He became the kind of friend I never thought I could have. After getting to know each other better within a short period, we decided to exchange numbers - surprisingly enough, it was Veron who asked for mine and I gladly gave it.

Days turned into weeks as we spent countless hours talking on the phone. Most of the time it would be him calling me; occasionally I would initiate the conversation as well. We discussed various topics such as studies, current events, our shared dislikes towards certain individuals, and so on. Veron always had something to talk about; in summary, it was mostly him speaking while I listened attentively. My mom had no objections to me being on the phone for long hours as long as she trusted me and I respected my boundaries - a promise I made to her. Academically, I consistently outperformed Veron. He had the potential to excel but never quite reached my level or met the teacher's expectations. I became more focused in class, diligently taking notes of important questions and lectures for future revision. We even had extra revision classes every Saturday for all students aiming for excellence. However, much to my delight (or perhaps disappointment), nobody could match my achievements; I always remained at the top of the class receiving high praise and commendations from most teachers. However, math posed a challenge for me - I would consistently score around 70%, which didn't satisfy my ambitions as a high achiever. Although I tried not to dwell on this too much and focused on other subjects instead, it felt unjust that math was holding me back.

ஐ

In the middle of sixth grade, we were informed about an incoming new student. Ellie and Veron engaged in a friendly debate with me about whether it would be a boy or a girl joining our class. Veron believed it would be another boy, while Ellie suggested that it might be someone who identified as transgender - she cleverly kept an open option just in case. Ellie truly enjoyed spending time with Veron too; we became like a tight-knit group of three individuals whose bond felt incredible.

Late one night, I found myself on a conference call with Veron and Ellie. "Heeeeey guysss!" I greeted enthusiastically.

"Heeeeyyyy!" Ellie responded with equal excitement.

Veron remained silent, causing me to wonder if he was even on the line.

"What's up? Is Veron part of this conference call? I can't seem to remember," I questioned.

"Yeah, maybe he's up to something he shouldn't be," Ellie speculated playfully. I giggled at her assumption.

"Eww! Stop making assumptions, Ellie." Veron finally spoke up, his voice sounding depressed. "Stop it, you two."

Concerned, Ellie asked him, "What's wrong? Are you okay?"

"Why do you care? It's not like you have anything to do with it," Veron burst out angrily.

I decided to stay quiet and observe the situation. Veron's response troubled me; something was bothering him. But why was he acting so cranky? I pushed that thought aside and put on my headphones before getting up from my bed to open the windows for some fresh air. Ellie refused to back down and asserted her right to know what was going on.

"Of course it makes me feel like I have something to do with it because of your reaction! What the hell happened?"

Veron dismissed her question with a curt reply: "Nothing... forget it! Stop acting like my mother." I rolled my eyes at his rude behaviour. What had gotten into him? Without warning, Ellie unleashed a string of censored words before abruptly ending the call by slamming her phone down in frustration. Sighing at my moody friends, I realized that now it was just Veron and my left on the line. The silence felt heavy as our breathing filled the background noise.

Finally breaking the silence, Veron whispered, "Say something."

Taking a deep breath myself, I responded, "I don't mind staying quiet. I just want you to know that I'm here for you when you're feeling down..."

"It's my dad..." Veron blurted out. "What about him?" I inquired, growing more curious.

"He has issues..." Veron trailed off.

"Regarding what?" I pressed for more information.

"He doesn't like it when I'm on the phone late at night, especially with a girl. I've tried so hard to make him understand that we're just friends, but it's been a struggle," Veron explained with frustration evident in his voice.

"I see," was all I could say, not fully grasping the situation.

"Don't make me continue," Veron pleaded. There was a hint of embarrassment in his voice as if he were blushing. I decided to remain silent and let him speak. A small smile formed on my face as he continued talking.

"Please don't give me the silent treatment again. It makes me nervous!" he pleaded with a touch of vulnerability in his voice.

"I make you nervous? Haha! That's surprising," I replied sarcastically, trying to lighten the mood.

"Yes, you do. At times, you can be quite intimidating and have a fiery temper. Your sensitive nature sometimes keeps me from doing certain things because I'm afraid of how you'll react. But despite it all, I love my best friend for who she is!" Veron confessed sincerely.

I remained quiet and fiddled with the wires of my headphones while staring at the wall in front of me. No response or answer would suffice; instead, fatigue began to set in as indicated by my small yawn.

"I'm feeling sleepy," I paused and took a deep breath before continuing, "and now isn't the right time for us to talk about this. Let's meet up at school..."

Veron immediately sensed a shift in my mood and apologized, "Are you upset by what I said? I'm sorry if it came across that way. I didn't mean to-"

I interrupted him abruptly, "This has nothing to do with you. I mean, I know who I am and what I'm about. It's just... never mind! Good night," I responded before ending the call. The next thing I knew, darkness enveloped me and sleep took over.

XV

Love Assignment

"Alright everyone, please take a seat," my English teacher announced.

I settled into my chair along with the rest of the class. Judging by the expression on our teacher's face, something exciting was about to happen or maybe she had some good news to share. Hopefully, it would be something positive. After dealing with all the exam stress lately, we could definitely use some good news to lighten our spirits. I glanced at Ellie and gave her a small smile in anticipation. In return, she gave me a look that seemed to say 'brace yourself for the worst.' I smirked and chuckled softly.

"Okay, it seems like everyone is quiet today," the teacher commented as she stood up from her desk and faced us all.

"I have an important announcement to make."

Anticipation filled the air as silence hung in anticipation of what she was about to reveal. The teacher continued after a brief pause, "As you all know, our 12th graders will be graduating this Friday and their parents along with other relatives are invited to attend. The girls will be wearing traditional saris while the boys will be dressed in tuxedos. On this day, we will bid farewell to our 12th graders and wish them luck in their future endeavours."

She paused again for a few seconds before looking at each one of us intently and added firmly, "So... I need each one of you to choose a partner from within the class and write or describe something related to romance or love. No excuses or complaints are allowed. Either complete this assignment or risk losing your grade..."

"Oh, this is going to be interesting," I thought to myself, excitement building up. "But I really want to get an A+ on this assignment!"

"I have already paired up the partners," my teacher announced with a wide smile.

"So, be prepared," she concluded. I couldn't help but flinch in my seat. My heart was already pounding loudly and my palms had turned cold.

"Here comes the nightmare," Ellie whispered in a mockingly horrified voice, making me even more nervous. "Get ready to face it."

Before my teacher could proceed with her announcement, a girl accompanied by the school peon entered the classroom.

"Miss, this is Danielle. She's a new admission... or rather a late admission! She recently moved here from another city due to her father's passing... Please make her feel welcome," the school peon informed my teacher in hushed tones that were still audible to us before leaving Danielle alone in the room. Her trembling hands and legs gave away her nervousness. Well, who isn't nervous on their first day of school? I vividly remember experiencing those jitters and feeling queasy as anxiety consumed me and made my stomach churn with uneasiness. It was an uncomfortable feeling we've all been through at some point. My teacher glanced at Danielle and offered her a small smile, which she returned albeit somewhat awkwardly. Shawn snickered mockingly nearby and I shot him a disapproving look.

"What?!?" he asked defiantly, meeting my gaze head-on. "

Where are your manners?" I whispered-yelled at him. He widened his eyes in surprise as I continued speaking softly, "Yeah, that's exactly what I've been wondering all this time..."

He opened his mouth as if about to respond but quickly closed it again. It looked like someone got irritated! Haha... what a shameless person!

"So..." my teacher began, turning her attention towards Danielle.

"Why don't you tell us a bit about yourself?" The entire class fell into a hushed silence as we focused our attention on her, eager to learn more. Meanwhile, I tried my best to observe every detail about her.

Starting, she had a distinct appearance with her glasses that screamed "NERD," even though she wasn't one. Her glasses gave off that impression. Her nose was small and could be described as a "button nose" by most writers. She had her hair messily tied into a bun, resembling tree branches hanging all over. As her bag swung to the right, I noticed her trembling and rubbing her sweaty palms, revealing the wetness on them. It was later revealed that she was dealing with mild mental retardation, having an IQ level equivalent to a 10-year-old while being in sixth grade where the average chronological age is 12. It was evident that she wasn't typical upon observation; it was not judgmental but merely stating the truth.

XVI
Confession

Veron sheepishly disclosed to me, "She admitted that she has a liking towards me."

Intrigued, I inquired, unaware of the identity of this mysterious "she,"

"Who is this 'she'?" He responded with a hint of embarrassment.

"Oh, come on... you're making me blush now." I widened my eyes and brought my phone closer to my ear.

Proceeding cautiously, I continued, "Are you referring to"

"Yes..." he replied.

I couldn't help but suppress a chuckle. "Well, it seems like you've caught yourself a crush there," I playfully teased.

With hesitation, he pondered before confessing, "Um... I

actually like her too..." This time my laughter escalated.

"What's so amusing? I reach out for your help and all I get is laughter. Guess I'll hang up then..." he jokingly remarked with mock sadness.

During that period, my true feelings towards him hadn't fully crystallized yet. It was still in the early stages of development. All I experienced were those fluttery sensations... tingles... and goosebumps whenever he spoke kindly about me! However, back then, I believed those emotions were just normal sentiments associated with growing up and not necessarily linked to romantic inclinations. Little did I know that they held deeper significance... well, emotional significance? At that moment, he was simply a friend in my eyes; nothing more than that. Eventually, my laughter subsided as I apologized sincerely.

"So tell me now, hero... what's the next move?" I inquired.

"Why would I have reached out to you if I already had everything planned?" he replied.

"True," I agreed and began contemplating.

"Well, both you and Danny have mutual feelings for each other. It's about time you listen to your heart's guidance. Your heart may physically reside on the left side of your chest, but it possesses an innate wisdom. Delve deep within yourself and ask the tough questions. Engage in a debate with your own thoughts until you discover an answer. Once you have that answer, follow it!"

"And that's precisely why I turn to you in these moments. You always know just what to say," he expressed his gratitude as butterflies fluttered in my stomach.

"Yeah, I guess I'm pretty remarkable," I modestly mumbled while gazing down at my feet. Why do I suddenly feel so bashful? It's not like he's standing right in front of me!

Expressing fondness for someone or having deep affection for them are distinct emotions. He stirred up my oxytocin, yet it was premature for me to grasp its significance. A sense of something existed within me, but was it merely infatuation or genuine love? I remain uncertain. I could feel a deep sense of tranquillity and warmth in my soul whenever I spent time with my friend. It was a truly delightful experience, filled with joy and contentment.

XVII
Sundays

On Sundays, people often have a chance to relax and unwind. It's a day when individuals can take a break from their usual routines and enjoy some leisure time. Whether it's spending quality time with family and friends, pursuing hobbies, or simply taking a walk in nature, Sundays offer the perfect opportunity to recharge and rejuvenate. One popular activity on Sundays is brunch. Many people indulge in a delicious meal that combines the best of breakfast and lunch. It's an enjoyable way to savour good food while catching up with loved ones. The laid-back atmosphere of brunch makes it even more appealing. Another common Sunday pastime is watching movies or binge-watching TV shows. It's a chance to escape into different worlds and immerse oneself in captivating stories. Whether it's a thrilling action film or a heartwarming romantic comedy, there are endless options to choose from. For those who enjoy outdoor activities, Sundays provide an ideal opportunity for exploration. Going for a hike in the mountains or taking a bike ride along scenic trails can be invigorating experiences. Connecting with nature not only benefits physical health but also brings peace of mind. Some people use Sundays as an opportunity for self-care and relaxation. Pampering oneself with spa treatments, reading a book by the fireplace, or simply taking a long bath can help alleviate stress and promote overall well-being. It's important to prioritize self-care and make time for rejuvenation. In conclusion, Sundays are precious days that allow individuals to recharge and focus on their well-being. Whether it involves spending quality time with loved ones, enjoying leisure activities, or practising self-care, everyone can find their way to make the most of this special day of the week.

When I think of Sundays, the first thing that comes to mind is the blissful opportunity for uninterrupted and long hours of sleep. After six consecutive days of early mornings and that groggy feeling upon waking up, Sunday is my chance to catch up on all the sleep I've been longing for. There's something heavenly about sinking into those silky covers and drifting off into a deep slumber. Why does the school have to start so early? Can't I just savour my precious sleep? It's a question that always lingers in my mind.

BEEP

The sound of my phone startled me from my drowsy state. I reached over to grab it and saw that I had received a message from an unknown number. Curiosity piqued, I tapped on the message to read it.

"Hello, I'm a thief and I am here to steal your heart."

I couldn't help but roll my eyes at the cheesiness of the

message. With slightly trembling hands, I typed out a response.

"I have no idea who you are. Care to introduce yourself?"

After hitting send, it only took twenty seconds for a reply to arrive.

Eagerly, I opened it. *"Hey, freaky red nose."*

A smile formed at the corners of my mouth as thoughts about this person crossed my mind. What an annoyingly amusing character!

"I'm sorry but it seems like my memory fails me when it comes to remembering cheesy individuals."

"Aww...you're so cute! Well, don't flatter yourself though. In my case, CUTE stands for 'C-causing U-unnecessary T-trouble E-everywhere.'"

"You'll never change,"

"I know"

I let out an exasperated sigh at this guy's predictable response.

Oh well! Now if you're wondering about the "Love Assignment," let me tell you that my teacher paired me up with none other than VERON! Talk about awkward, right? Tyler got paired with Danny, and Shawn with Ellie. Kris was the odd one out as there wasn't a girl available in our class to partner with him. So the teacher assigned him a solo performance for his assignment. He was thrilled when he found out he didn't have a partner. Jealousy, much? Yeah, I admit it. I wished I could be the only one too. It would've been easier that way.

"Do you have any ideas for our assignment?" I asked Veron.

"Yes," he replied, gazing tenderly into my eyes, "We should write about romantic love."

"Really?" I quipped with interest and continued playfully, "Go on."

He blinked and began speaking softly while still maintaining eye contact, "Love is looking into her eyes and knowing that's where you always want to be—lost in her loving gaze...and wanting nothing more than to embrace her tightly, knowing she'll feel safe in your arms and feeling like the luckiest person alive." He leaned closer as he spoke, "Love is feeling her warm breath sending shivers down your spine and never wanting to let go of that sensation." He smiled warmly, "Love is selflessly sacrificing your own desires for the happiness of the other person because you know deep down that she will always be there for you." He looked down briefly before continuing, "But not everyone is fortunate when it comes to love. Many relationships end in tragedy or heartbreak due to disloyalty. Love is patient. Love is kind. Love is like losing your mind. But in the beginning, it is blind. In the end, it is divine," He met my gaze again and concluded his thoughts.

"Wow," I said, keeping my eyes locked on his.

He smirked playfully and asked me teasingly, "So what do you think about it?"

"What do I think?" I mocked, playfully widening my eyes.

I marvelled at the breathtaking, awe-inspiring conclusion of the piece. "Love is patient. Love is kind. Love is like losing your mind. But in the beginning, it is blind. In the end, it is divine," I recited slowly and softly, appreciating its poetic rhyming scheme. "You have a talent for words," I complimented.

"Yeah...I'm not so sure," he replied, sounding uncertain.

"Why not? You're perfect.."

"Perfect? No one truly is. I'm far from it," he confessed.

"Perfection isn't about being an expert in something. Perfection," I pointed to my heart, "comes from within."

As the year drew to a close, it was time for the results to be announced. My mother was astonished, overjoyed, and amazed when she saw my report card after completing 6th grade - 99%! Her happiness knew no bounds. It was fulfilling to finally find a way to make my mother proud and see her so delighted. The best part was that I felt on top of the world; I had never been this happy before. If only my father were here to share this news with him...but he was travelling abroad. If only he knew... During a parent-teacher meeting at school to discuss report cards, My teacher informed my mom about areas where I needed special attention in mathematics but expressed confidence that with focused effort, I could excel in it as well.

"Rene needs to give special attention to mathematics and I am sure she will excel. She can do better with a little more concentrated effort. She is a humble girl, and I have trust in her that she can do better in Mathematics."

Hearing this made me want to hide away and disappear forever. I would rather suffer alone than deal with math. Please, I beg you, no more math. I despise numbers. Please. Can someone hear me? Can anyone hear my cries and pleas? My brain feels like it's about to burst. I'm on the verge of exploding any minute. I know, so dramatic, right? Yes, I admit it. I can be quite a drama queen.

Soon enough, we got to know about Danny. Speaking of her personality, she had an average appearance and some unpleasant habits. Silent theft and manipulation were her defining traits. She also had a bad odor and her school shoes emitted such a terrible stench that being near her was unbearable. Her handwriting and academic performance were dreadful, making her unpopular with the teachers. However, she did have one redeeming quality - she was friendly and sometimes even helpful! Her laughter was contagious; it never failed to bring a smile to your face. Gradually, I discovered that Elena had feelings for Shawn. She confessed when she believed it to be true. I couldn't help but wonder what she saw in him! He was such a rebellious troublemaker. But then again, don't most girls find bad boys attractive? Well, I prefer good-natured innocent boys myself! Yes, I'm different! It feels refreshing to stand out rather than blend in with the crowd. Shawn,

Danny, and Kris were the only ones who didn't take their studies seriously. They treated it as a mere pastime. They believed that passing exams was all that mattered. Good grades were not part of their vocabulary matter how much effort we put into helping them excel, it simply didn't happen. It seemed like achieving at least 75% would remain nothing more than wishful thinking for them. Just like any other teenager experiencing crushes, summer flings, and admiration for cute boys, I too developed feelings of attraction towards handsome young men. It was merely infatuation, a fleeting fancy; nothing as serious as love.

When it comes to crushes, I've had my fair share. I've been attracted to many people throughout my life. It's interesting how just a glimpse of them walking by can ignite a spark of admiration in our eyes, causing us to tremble with excitement. They say that eyes speak volumes, and you can truly see the whole story behind someone's eyes. Sometimes, we even escape into a fantasy world where we imagine all sorts of things with that special person. Things that we never thought could happen suddenly become possible in this imaginary realm. Ah, the wonders of puberty! It truly makes us feel like we're going crazy, doesn't it? Our hormones go haywire and our emotions run wild.

During most of my summer break, I stayed at my aunt's house. If there's one person who I consider as my role model, it would be my aunt. She happens to be my mom's sister and she is an incredible source of inspiration and light in my life. She brings me so much happiness and love. She has always been there for me every step of the way, ready to pick me up when I fall (sometimes after having a good laugh). She is not only an aunt but also a best friend

- someone who understands me on a deep level. We are so alike that at times I even mistake her for my sister. You could say that I am a combination of both my mom and dad's traits as well as hers - religiosity, spirituality, equality - these are some qualities that define who I am. Isn't it fascinating how certain traits manifest differently in each member of a family? Especially the good ones! It's quite rare to see these days - those genuinely good qualities. I always knew that whenever I needed advice or guidance, I could turn to her without hesitation. Her presence alone made me feel comfortable enough to talk about anything and everything with her. Having her by my side was truly a blessing. She played multiple roles in my life - a best friend, a sister, a mother figure, and of course, an aunt.

Have you ever had someone who could be so many personalities to you but all wrapped up in one body? Well, I certainly did! I consider myself incredibly lucky to have so many significant people condensed into one person. During my time spent with my aunt that summer, she shared religious stories and spoke about spirituality - something that my mother never really discussed. My mother believed in the essence of good karma - being good to receive goodness in return. Religiosity wasn't a big part of her vocabulary.

She would occasionally go to church, but only on rare occasions - maybe two or three times every six months. She believed that God was omnipresent and didn't feel the need to go to church specifically to pray. Coming from that background, I held similar beliefs as well. However, under the influence of my aunt's teachings, I started seeing the importance of attending mass more frequently and participating in faith formation activities. According to her perspective, God has given us life and we must sing praises and express gratitude for this gift. My aunt also emphasized the concept of equality. She taught me that everyone is equal because, at our core, we are all human beings.

True richness doesn't come from material possessions such as vast lands or expensive belongings; it comes from within ourselves - our character and how we treat others. Kindness and helpfulness are what truly make us rich individuals deserving of respect both for ourselves and from others. Our worthiness stems from our personality rather than what we possess materially. Richness isn't synonymous with perfection; it lies within our hearts and souls instead of material possessions. In short, when we do good deeds and treat others well, we automatically become rich in spirit. Those artificial things like fancy cars or expensive clothes are fleeting, but the impact of our good actions will be remembered forever. This realization truly caught me off guard. Her words and stories served as a constant inspiration to me, and I plan to pass down these valuable lessons to my future children. I could go on and on about the other things she taught me, but I believe it's best to conclude here.

XVIII

My True Feelings

Time flew by and before I knew it, I had reached 8th grade. It was during this period that I discovered my true feelings for my closest companion. He was always there for me, especially in times of need. When I lost my father, he provided comfort and reassurance, making my world feel perfect. Just his presence alone was enough to make me forget about everything else. There were moments when I could sense that he wanted to embrace me and alleviate the pain, but his shyness held him back. It always made me laugh when I thought about it - he could be quite timid at times. However, despite all this, we never embraced each other. Perhaps both of us were too shy. It's amazing how contagious shyness can be sometimes, isn't it? Deep down, though, what I yearned for was a hug from him - a hug that would convey the message "Everything will be alright; I'm here for you." Unfortunately, that moment never came to pass. Furthermore, there were instances when he would say the sweetest things to me that left me feeling overwhelmed with emotions. Those jokes... oh boy! They had the power to make me burst into laughter uncontrollably. I am truly grateful for all the times he stood by my side without wavering. Eventually, what started as mere "liking" transformed into something much deeper - love.

You see, I never expected to fall in love with my best friend; such things seemed more fitting in movies or cheesy romance novels than in real life. But these feelings were completely natural; they weren't influenced by teenage love stories or clichéd romantic movies - they just happened on their own accord. Is this something everyone goes through? Is it a common symptom? Does having a crush indicate an underlying condition? Could it be love? Can love be contagious? And is it truly impossible for a guy and girl to maintain a strictly platonic friendship? So many questions flooded my mind all at once. I needed a break from this incessant pondering. "Love is patient, love is kind. Love is like losing your mind. In the beginning, it blinds; in the end, it becomes divine." Of course, my foolish brain couldn't help but hear his voice! It sends shivers down my spine every single time his words echo in my head. Why did things have to turn out this way? What did puberty do to me? Why me? I used to believe that losing the love of your life was the most painful experience one could endure. Just like how breakups can be excruciatingly painful, it hurts even more when you realize that the person you love is completely oblivious to your feelings. Love is a crazy and peculiar sensation - it makes butterflies flutter in your stomach, causes goosebumps on your hands and legs, and sends those nervous tremors down your spine, leaving you feeling slightly dazed and queasy. Yes, I know what it feels like to love someone deeply, but having that affection unrequited is an even more agonizing ordeal. That's what they call "one-sided love," which eventually morphed into a crushing feeling known as a "crush." It truly felt as though my heart had been crushed and trampled upon. It was utterly heartbreaking! What happened next? Did I curl up into a ball, clutching my knees while sinking into depression? Oh yes, indeed! I experienced my first heartbreak firsthand. People always told me that crying over a boy was the silliest mistake one could make, but little did I know that there was no other choice for me but to succumb to tears. Why waste precious tears on someone who never reciprocates those feelings? It would be an utter waste of time and energy. Besides, he was already in a relationship with Danny, so why should I even bother? Oh, please note the sarcasm when I say "bother."

The mere thought of Veron and Danny together always tugged at my heartstrings, causing a profound ache. The weight of heartbreak, depression, and regret seemed unbearable. It was an overwhelming amount of emotional turmoil to process. However, it was time to move forward. After all, I have a life to live, dreams to pursue, and countless places to explore. I refuse to be defined as "the girl who succumbed to depression." I will persevere, even in the face of losing the love of my life. I will remain strong and stand tall.

By the way, did I mention that Shane and Kris transferred schools? It came as news to me when Ellie informed me about it. Speaking of Elena, she has been my unwavering support throughout this ordeal. She has stood by my side like a courageous soldier, defending me when necessary. Our friendship has taught me the true meaning of loyalty and companionship. I am immensely grateful for her role in shaping me into a better person. As time went on, Veron and Danny's love blossomed while my feelings for Veron continued to burn within me. Nights were spent cocooned in my blanket with tears streaming down my face as I hoped he would realize the depth of my love for him. At times, the pain became so overwhelming that self-inflicted wounds seemed like an escape route; however, I learned to endure it and accept that perhaps destiny had something better in store for me. Falling in love is an indescribable sensation that defies words or explanations. You just know it when you feel it deep within your soul. If you were to ask me what it feels like precisely... Well, words would fail me miserably trying to capture its essence for you. All I can say is that it is both the most incredible feeling imaginable and simultaneously the most agonizing one too. It's like being on cloud nine, where life couldn't possibly be any better. But it's also akin to being struck by an enormous truck, where you can taste, smell, and feel the presence of death. I could elaborate on these contradictory emotions endlessly, but I won't. What I will tell you is that love is inescapable. No matter how hard you try to resist its pull, it will always find a way to exist within your heart. It doesn't matter how many trains you board, how many cities you traverse, or how many miles you travel; love will persist.

I used to invite Veron and Danny over to my place every month. Veron got along well with my brother, and even my mom approved of him as a good guy. On one such occasion, the three of us decided to head up to one of the rented houses in my building for some privacy. As we settled in there together, lying down comfortably, something unexpected happened - Veron ended up on my lap! To say I was taken aback would be an understatement; however, I refrained from blurting out any expletives. Was this reality or just a dream? If it was indeed a dream, please don't wake me up; let me revel in this blissful illusion for as long as possible. Could he sense the rapid pounding of my heart? It feels like it's about to burst out of my chest at any moment. Relax...this should be relaxing...right? As I examined him closely at that moment, suddenly everything became clear - his charm and magnetism that other girls had noticed all along. How could I have been so blind for the past three years? My affection for him grew deeper with each passing second. Should I confess my feelings or keep them hidden away? Oh, dear...I desperately needed some guidance here! Divya remained oblivious to the situation as if she couldn't see Veron on my lap. How foolish and naïve! I yearned to kiss him, to feel his presence against me. But with Danny's presence, any such possibility was out of the question. If only I could freeze time at that very moment... What was he thinking at that very instant? However, one question continued to plague my mind - what did it mean to him when he lay on my lap? Did he have feelings for me too?

Are we such close pals that it's normal for us to go through this? I don't think he would be interested in me, who has low self-esteem and feels unattractive. There's something amiss with me, I've never experienced love before, but I was head over heels for him. I needed to confide in someone. Maybe I should have a chat with my mom? Nah, I'll get some random advice on how young love is immature. Maybe Reynold? Nah, he doesn't believe in love. Ugh! I don't have anyone else. That night, I made up my mind to reach out to Ellie and ask her to come over the next day. She came right away and lent an ear as I bared my soul. I told her that being around him only intensified my feelings for him, and at this point in my life, I didn't want to be in a relationship!

"So...you're saying you...don't want to be friends with Veron? With us?" Ellie asked curiously.

"No...I just need some space from Veron...to figure things out for myself," I explained.

This was something Veron would never find out.

"What do you mean?" she asked puzzledly. "I mean...I need some time alone before talking to Veron again. I'm afraid if we talk now, I'll break down all over again. So, I need your help. I want you guys not to talk or contact me", I said frustratedly

"Ignore him? How can we help with that?" she questioned.

"Just avoid talking or interacting with me. Let Veron know that I'm not in the mood for any conversation.I blurted it out."

"You're in love with him. But, you won't admit it. What's the problem, Rene? He's a great guy and he cares about you so much," she pointed out.

"I can't allow myself to fall in love with him...I'm scared Danny...I just can't," I confessed. "Besides, he was with Danny short term and I wouldn't want to jeopardize our friendship."

"You're already in love. Don't lie to yourself," she said, trying to make me see the truth.

"I don't know what I'm doing with my life...What have I become, Ellie? Why am I so lost? I want to be happy, but I'm afraid of happiness. I'm afraid of love. I'm afraid of trust. I'm afraid of losing," I sobbed uncontrollably.

"I didn't want to hurt him, but that was the only way to make him hate me."

"Why are you doing this to yourself?" Ellie asked, holding my head gently.

"I hate seeing you hurt. Why are you running away? Life can be tough sometimes, but not always. Give him a chance. Tell him everything." She gave me a reassuring look.

"I can't..." I looked away.

No way that could happen. Now, I'll be alone and try to find myself again. I officially announced our group's breakup. It's me who will break us apart. With that thought in mind, I rushed home. I didn't want to see or talk to anyone anymore. It was late as I made my way home. It had been one of the worst days ever. The person whom I've liked since 8th grade now disgusted me. So it turns out that for three and a half years, all those feelings were for nothing. How pathetic am I? And on top of it all, he never even knew how much he meant to me. Sitting alone in my room with tears streaming down my face, hours went by as the pain consumed me. How did things end up like this? Throughout 9th grade, I completely ignored him. In the end, though, I couldn't bear it anymore. I wanted to talk to him. My mind was filled with questions but he wasn't there to answer them!!! Maybe I wasn't meant for him after all. I pondered over that thought, but eventually sighed and gave up.

When life isn't picture-perfect,
When things don't fall into place,
When everything starts to fade,
When you have nothing left to embrace,

Gazing into the mirror, Unable to identify flaws,
Feeling like your world has crumbled and shattered,
Don't be afraid, my friend!

These are common occurrences in life's journey,
Sadness, misery, pain, and heartbreak are inevitable.
It's all part of the intricate cycle of existence,
So don't relinquish hope, for when you do, life loses its essence.

Learn to cherish the little joys that surround you,
For they hold immense significance in this vast world.
Focus on what brings you happiness and contentment,
And banish thoughts of unhappiness from your mind.

Oh dear God, I humbly beseech you for two things: love and happiness.
I implore you to illuminate my life with the radiance of joy.
Having witnessed sorrow, suffering, and torment both physical and mental,
I yearn for genuine happiness. Please bestow it upon me.

Eradicate every trace of sadness from my being.
Let pain become a distant memory that no longer haunts me.
Secondly, I request your divine intervention in matters of love.
May I experience unconditional love from those around me;
May they appreciate me for who I am rather than material

possessions.

Lord, these two desires are all I seek from you;
Nothing artificial or superficial is desired.
Grant me the light of love and happiness in my existence;
Illuminate my path so that sadness never engulfs me again.

In the depths of despair, refrain from inflicting harm upon yourself. Even during your most trying moments, resist the urge to end your own life. Despite feeling worthless, unloved, unwanted, and uncared for, there is someone out there for whom you mean everything. You may not be aware of it, but I assure you that the person least expected to fall in love with you is head over heels for you. If you were to take your own life, you would also be taking away their reason for living. They would suffer immeasurable pain without the privilege of witnessing your smile and gazing upon your beautiful face each day. Therefore, before succumbing to self-inflicted harm, take a moment to contemplate who would truly care about your well-being. Additionally, bear in mind that your scars contribute to shaping the unique individual that you are. We all bear scars both internally and externally. These scars may manifest as freckles caused by sun exposure or emotional triggers resulting from past experiences. They can also be physical through broken bones or emotional through heartbreaks. However these scars manifest within us, there should be no shame attached to them; instead, they should be celebrated as a testament to our strength and resilience. You possess an inherent beauty that transcends any external factors such as background, appearance, material possessions or societal standards. Regardless of your height, weight, gender identity, ethnicity or religion - regardless of the colour of your skin or who you love - know that without a doubt you are stunningly beautiful and this truth should never be questioned or doubted by anyone - including yourself.

As I daydreamed about my aspirations, the thought of visiting the Eiffel Tower and experiencing my first kiss filled me with excitement. The idea of strolling into Buckingham Palace and momentarily feeling like a queen added to the allure. And who wouldn't want to have a lively dance night at a pub in New York? Lastly, indulging in authentic Chinese cuisine while being in China would be an unforgettable experience.

"My dear, you need not dwell on the past. You should understand by now that nothing lasts forever. People come and go as though it's an open-door policy. You have a life of your own now, so live it to the fullest," she advised with a gentle tone.

"Yes, you're right, Mom," I resolved with determination in my voice.

Being unloved is a truly terrible experience, especially when the reasons behind it remain unclear. People hurl hurtful words at you, leaving you bewildered and lost. Consequently, you begin scrutinizing every perceived flaw within yourself. You strive to improve and appear "normal." However, even if you give it your all, your efforts often end in disappointment, leaving you feeling utterly shattered. The overwhelming pain becomes too much to bear, and tears offer no solace as they should. You may have heard that releasing emotions helps alleviate the agony, so you cry and cry in hopes of finding relief. Yet, the pain persists relentlessly. It refuses to fade away or let you forget what happened and why it left you feeling so broken. In such moments of despair, everyone seeks their way to cope with the anguish. Allowing yourself to cry is perfectly acceptable; shedding tears can serve as a cathartic release for your pent-up emotions. Just let it all out without holding back. Afterwards, reach out to your closest friends for uplifting conversations that will help lift your spirits significantly.

Remember that time plays a crucial role in healing wounds like these. Experiencing heartbreak for the first time is an inevitable part of life's journey—a shared experience felt by countless others around the world. Acknowledging this fact allows you to mourn appropriately without letting it consume your entire day or define who you are as a person—a sense of self-pity only hinders progress. Perhaps this is merely an aspect of growing up—when we're young, we console ourselves with phrases like "If it didn't work out, then it wasn't meant to be," simply because they sound comforting on the surface. We naively believe that something just as wonderful awaits us around the next corner in life's unpredictable path. However, true connections are rare and uniquely special; bidding farewell to something that meant everything shouldn't be taken lightly or dismissed as insignificant. Just because you will eventually heal and move on doesn't mean you should simply let go without fully understanding the weight of saying goodbye to something so significant.

Thank You, My Reader.

I am grateful that you have chosen to embark on the journey of reading my book. It is my sincerest hope that this experience has been truly transformative for you. My intention in sharing my story was to ignite a flame of hope within the hearts of readers, reminding them that even in the darkest moments, there is always a glimmer of light at the end of the tunnel. I would greatly appreciate your feedback on my book and would be honored if you could share your own personal experiences with me. By doing so, I can empathize with your struggles and share in your pain. Thank you for investing in my book; it means more to me than words can express. I am currently working on my second book, and I invite you to stay connected with me through all of my social media platforms. Rest assured, I will notify you as soon as my next literary creation becomes available. In order to make a greater impact and bring solace to more individuals trapped in their own miseries, I kindly ask for your support in spreading the word about my book. Together, we can reach countless souls and offer them a lifeline towards healing and salvation.

In case you ever feel like reaching out, feel free to drop me an email at renesamuel1996@gmail.com. Don't hesitate to share your tales or struggles; let's journey through this path of healing together. You can also find me on Instagram @renesam96 and my book @unsaid_goodbye_bookbyerene for further engagement and updates on my upcoming literary projects.

www.ingramcontent.com/pod-product-compliance
Lightning Source LLC
LaVergne TN
LVHW091051150826
845673LV00002B/545